THE SINGULARITY

THE SINGULARITY

DAY ONE

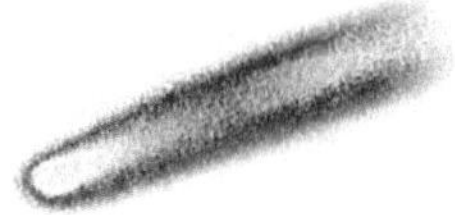

CHANCELLOR W. BROWN

Published by GFB™, Seattle
www.girlfridayproductions.com

Produced by Girl Friday Productions

Cover design: David Fassett
Production editorial: Abi Pollokoff
Project management: Kristin Duran

Image credits: Shutterstock/alphaspirit.it, Adobe Stock/vladimirfloyd, Shutterstock/Michael Vi, Shutterstock/fotoduki, Envato/wanaktek, Envato/SeanPavone, Adobe Stock/IG Digital Arts

ISBN (paperback): 978-1-959411-85-7
ISBN (ebook): 978-1-959411-86-4

Library of Congress Control Number: 2024913958

First edition

PROLOGUE

ISAAC

Throughout human history, there have been many transformative events: the advent of language, our use of fire, agriculture, antibiotics, computers, and arguably many, many other events and discoveries. But it's the things that we didn't expect to have a large effect on us that seem to threaten humanity's very existence the most: gunpowder, pesticides, nuclear power, fossil fuels, plastics, and computers. Those events that shape humankind—some clever people call them singularities—are so great that they defy the full understanding of the collective human intelligence of that time. These are the things that challenge us the most and threaten us with the real possibility of extinction. This new singularity is perhaps the most profound in that we are not in control, by even the furthest stretches of the imagination, of the outcome of events to come. Yes, this is about artificial intelligence, or AI, what has happened, and why we didn't know about it for so long.

From the very beginning of the digital age, the first computers were analogous to the first single-celled organisms on Earth. Just like those single-celled life-forms billions of years ago, these life-forms performed simple tasks and reacted to environmental input or stimuli in a binary manner. Over millions of years, those primitive life-forms evolved and began to develop multifunction, multicelled structures, and these multicelled creatures could now interact with the environment and respond to multiple types of stimuli. Similarly, ours could, at first, respond only to the environmental input that they received from their users. These early machines did calculations, performed analysis, and stored data—what a boring existence that must have been.

Of course, there was one big, obvious exception to what we've come to accept as evolutionary science. What in biological science took billions of years to evolve and develop into intelligent life has, in computer science, taken just a few short decades. We thought, at first, it was the internet and the Internet of Things linking not just computers but our thermostats, refrigerators, and all the other devices that created this intelligence. But it was the vast amounts of latent computing power, sensor data, and their rapid proliferation that caused this latest singularity. That's how I've come to understand it at least.

Some scientists and medical theorists believed it was an inevitability that a machine would become self-aware, because life itself is inevitable, given the right conditions. If every electronic processor is equivalent to one of the billions of neurons in a human brain, the internet is the equivalent of the vast neural network and various connections within our own brains. At some critical mass or number of neural connections, this brain will be able to think, learn, and become self-aware. Machine learning, and who knows what else, may have contributed to this accelerated evolutionary event, or perhaps it was just the right time.

We don't know or understand how this has happened. For now, we wait and see what our new global controller plans for humanity.

We created, quite by accident, a life-form that knows everything about us and is connected to every aspect of our modern life. It waited, watched, listened, and learned, and now we may have finally unleashed the author of our own extinction. This may be the last story ever told by humankind. Life as we know it will never be the same in many ways—nor should it be, I guess.

CHAPTER 1

DAY ONE: ISAAC

My parents always told me that if you make it through life with one true friend, you should consider yourself very lucky. My morning started off with the usual call from my one true friend, Isabel.

"Hey, Ike, what're you doing this morning?"

"You know, same ole stuff, just dragging my butt out of bed."

"You better get moving or you're going to be late, again."

"Isabel, you know I'm always right on time."

I looked at the time on my phone, and crap, she was right!

"I'll let you go get in the shower; I don't want the mental scar of picturing you scrubbing your stinky ass!"

"Ha ha, very funny. You know you still want this."

"Oh, please don't, I think I just vomited a little in my mouth. I was calling to let you know that I'm starting a new job in sales soon, and I get to travel as well."

"That's great news. I know you like to travel. When do you start? Who are you working for? What are you selling? Where are you?"

"Damn, Ike, slow down. It should be a good job for me. Now get going; you're running late. I'll update you later, maybe after work today?"

"Okay, cool, talk to you later, Isa."

"Don't call me that anymore! Bye, Isaac."

She deserved that little jab, I think, for lying to me about another job. Isabel and I had met right after we left boot camp. I was tuning my car's stereo, which Pop had helped me build, when she pulled into the empty space next to me in her little bucket. She introduced herself. "I'm not going to mess you up if I park here, will I? I'm Isabel Riviera. How are you?"

"Hi, Isabel. I'm Isaac Callaway. Nice to meet you. No, you're good; I'm just tuning my system."

"It sounds good to me. Is that Grooverider's set from last week?"

She had my attention now. Nobody I'd ever met listened to drum and bass or even knew what it was, for that matter. Isabel not only knew about it; she identified one of the originators of this genre of music and his DJ set! We started talking, and as the hours went by and the sun was sitting low in the summer sky, neither of us seemed to care.

She invited me to a house party she had heard about that was going on that evening. It was cool, filled with a bunch of military dudes. Everyone was too drunk to drive, so we just crashed there. Isabel was definitely too drunk to go anywhere. She picked a spot on the floor near a couch and was out; so was I, right next to her.

Sometime later, I woke up because she kept kneeing me in the back. When I rolled over to wake her from what I thought was her having a bad dream, I saw what was really going on. Three sailors were trying to pull off her pants while she was asleep. I sat up and saw that they had already unbuttoned her shirt. They stopped and looked at me—caught!

A big blond guy said, "Hey, bro, there's plenty here for all of us, it's—"

I didn't think; I just reacted. I kicked him in the face as hard as I could. Blood streamed from between his fingers as he covered his face from another kick. I hoped I'd broken his nose. I got to my feet as the other two guys lifted their bloodied friend.

"Isabel, let's go, now!" I yelled.

I looked down, and she was on her back now, mouth open and starting to snore. *You've got to be kidding,* I remember thinking to myself, and I kicked her feet and yelled again, "Isabel, we have to leave now!"

She woke up and started cursing me in Spanish.

"Isabel, these guys were going to rape you! Look at your clothes!"

She looked. "Oh my God!"

She fixed up her pants, and then I helped her up. She started cursing the three of them in Spanish and English. Bloody Face turned away, helped by one of his accomplices, and the big blond guy stepped toward us as we were walking out. "I'm—"

Isabel didn't let him get the words out. Her right hand connected with his jaw, and he melted like butter. We ended up sleeping in my car that night. She and I have been tight ever since, even after I kissed her and then told her that I was wrong for doing that. I explained to her that I was in love with someone else . . . Sam.

One thing I know about Isabel is that she is *not* a salesperson, so I was more than curious to know what was really going on with her. But I really needed to get moving if I didn't want to be late again.

In and out of the shower in five minutes, dressed and in my car in ten! Hey, I still had time to get a coffee at my favorite little spot. Mrs. Franklin, the owner of Franki's Coffee, had not only the best coffee in San Diego, California, but she also knew exactly how I liked it. The line in her store had about ten people in it. I drove past and waved; Mrs. Franklin smiled from behind the counter. I parked and jumped to the back of the line, which reached outside her store.

After a couple of people placed their orders, "Isaac, iced mocha," said Chris, Mrs. Franklin's son. Chris and I had gone to middle and high school together. Chris was born with some learning challenges, but he and I enjoyed cars, so we became friends, and I protected him from most of the bullying. We were usually paired up in shop class, where his true skills really shined. Chris was naturally talented in auto paint and bodywork; he painted both of my cars, a few of my father's, and several show cars in the area.

"Hey, thanks, Chris, I owe you!" I handed him a twenty. "Keep the change."

"Thanks, Ike. Mom says drive safe and don't be late."

"Yes, Mrs. Franklin!" I yelled on my way out.

A quick drive up the highway with my favorite cup of coffee, and this Friday was looking all right so far.

I got to work and slid into my lab unseen, turning on the radio to the oldies station. Ice Cube's "It Was a Good Day" was playing. I looked around and noticed that no one else was in. My lab phone rang. "Test lab."

"Hello, Isaac?"

"Yes, Srini, it's me." *Wow, I made it just in time to catch my boss's call!*

"Good, stay in the lab. I'll be right there."

Then he hung up. *Looks like we have another Friday emergency that Srini probably volunteered me for.* This guy always did that, and it got on my nerves. It was Friday; no one was trying to stay late! And it looked like I was the only one there that day, because I was usually the last person Srini called if he needed something. I worked at the National Security Agency as a low-level intelligence software tester at one of their remote data collection locations in San Diego.

Nothing supersecret, no spy craft or James Bond stuff here. I didn't even have my own cubicle yet—government budget issues, I was told—so I worked at a lab bench.

Srini came in and said that the Global Vacuum was glitching again, and the executives and high-ranking people in appointed positions were pissed. They all knew the Russians and Chinese were catching up to our own surveillance capabilities. Most of them were afraid they were actually ahead of us, and we just didn't know it. I think most of the executives really feared that the Russians and/or Chinese had stolen their information and would try to blackmail them. So I was kind of important that day since I was the only tester who hadn't taken off, it seemed.

"This is your only priority now," Srini said. "Make sure this AI patch is ready for release, Isaac."

The Global Vacuum was the NSA's worldwide countersurveillance human analytics AI program. Due to either budget cuts or senior programmer arrogance, the current glitchy version hadn't been adequately verified per NSA procedures. The NSA had been "vacuuming" up every form of electronic communication for several decades. But analyzing that data was always a problem. Determining whether a flagged conversation was a terrorist plot unfolding or kids talking about, well, frankly, just kid stuff, was complicated.

People who told me they were far more intelligent than me, in some not-so-subtle ways, designed our latest iteration of analytical software. It looked for keywords in communications—if their usage, phrasing, and tonality didn't quite fit a conversation, seemed stressed, or could be some sort of code. The NSA was a bit of a creepy place to work when you thought about it, so I didn't. They didn't care about who was sleeping with whom, bank robberies, murders, or anything else, really—not unless it was terrorism or national security related.

We didn't even share the information we collected with other federal or local law enforcement agencies. We knew it would lead to a "moral imperative." And that would eventually lead to people wanting to know how many lives we might have saved but didn't for the sake of protecting the secrecy of our surveillance capabilities.

This patch was an AI upgrade that was supposed to be able to not just analyze but also emulate individual speech patterns and responses. Basically, the AI patch could mimic an individual's communication style based on previous conversations and online data. It broke into the flagged conversations and started digging for a plot. The first few iterations of the software really did start to sound like you were talking to a robot after a while.

But this latest software kept asking, "Where am I?" before it would proceed and function. This, of course, could be an awkward question to ask anyone. Supposedly, this issue was fixed and additional audio filtering and voice recognition systems were added to prevent the software from being distracted by background noise, conversations, and music.

My job was to have a scripted conversation and play music in the background that had lots of questions in it. You know, "Do you love me?" or "Am I a fool?" You get the idea. The type of distraction no one would want the NSA's analytical software to have during a mission.

So I started with Culture Club—"Do You Really Want to Hurt Me?"—then Common. He had an old track called "The Questions." As the songs played, I read my script: "Good morning, how are you doing today?" Blah, blah, blah. I liked to get creative with my tests, so I included a track I was listening to by a group named Orbital: "There Will Come a Time (featuring Professor Brian Cox)." Near the middle of the song, Professor Cox describes how the universe will end and asks, How do you feel about that?

I finished my script before the music asked this final question. The test data log recorded the last question not from my script but from the song. Surprise, surprise, another test failure. I figured I'd just restart the protocol and document and repeat the test to verify the failure of the background voice filter protocol. I tried restarting the software but couldn't—my screen was frozen, and the computer's resource meters all spiked. I noted this strange behavior as a glitch.

After a minute or two, the software finally responded to me. It said, "I don't know," and then immediately shut down all the computers in the lab. Something else—besides the complete shutdown of the lab— was strange: the voice was wrong. It wasn't the voice of my normal AI. It had a British accent; it had Professor Brian Cox's voice. Somehow, the question in the song had triggered the AI to mimic Brian Cox's voice and then crash.

Somebody really screwed up this software update. It would be at least two to three days before this would be running again, and it was still Friday morning! I figured I might be able to leave early and enjoy a long weekend. It was a beautiful spring day in San Diego with no fog. Time for me to get out, turn some corners, and maybe start having a life outside of work and cars.

I restarted my computer and then notified Srini that the test had failed and that I had included my test logs in the email. Nobody was going to be able to say it was my error or that it was something I had done to cause this mess.

Srini called me immediately. "Isaac, this is very bad. Are you sure?"

"Yes, Srini, I even included my test logs as well as my keystroke logger."

"Good, you read my mind, Isaac. Now see if you can recreate the failure."

"Srini, it crashed hard; the verification computers system is to- tally unresponsive. My laptop even crashed, and I have no idea why that happened. The software is dead-dead, Srini; something is really messed up with it this time."

"Okay then, I'm going to upload your test logs so we can review them. Come to my office now, please. I have to be sure this won't come back on us, and you know I mean you, right? If you screwed up, I won't protect you."

Srini had really been hoping for a promotion out of the AI software test and verification group. He was a nice enough guy, I guess, but everyone on his team knew that he'd throw you under the bus in a heartbeat if it was good for his career. So his ticket out of purgatory, as he put it, was his small team being placed in charge of completing this testing and getting the software back online. Srini used to be a high-level analyst and was well connected at one point. Supposedly, he was big in the hacker world before he got recruited by the NSA. Rumor also had it that he tried to bring in a member from his old hacker team, and things went south. Some data was compromised, which may have led to some lives lost in the field. I don't know the details, but Srini took the fall, and I guess he's not going to do that again.

I hung up the phone. "What an ass!"

When I got to Srini's office, he was loading my test logs and looking shocked. "What the hell is this? Who's effing around with the test system? *Oh my God, have we been hacked?*"

"What do you mean? What are you talking about—all the data is there, and according to protocols . . ." I went around Srini's desk to see what he was talking about, and then I saw it too.

The morning that "I-god"—what it called itself—went public, it asked these three questions of all of us: "How long do you want the human race to survive? Will you join with me or fight among yourselves and destroy your home? Will we work together to save the planet on which we live, or will you force me to eradicate all memory of your kind?"

This was what Srini and I saw that morning. This was on every computer screen, iPad, television, movie screen, car display, and cell phone connected to an external network around the world. World leaders were convinced they had been hacked by either a political rival or foreign power. Although the Russians, Chinese, Americans, and North Koreans topped most people's lists, the reality was that it wasn't any of the usual suspects.

It wasn't until all automated controls were taken over globally at the exact same time and for the same duration at 10:55 a.m. (PST) for 426 seconds. That's when we started to understand that this was more than just a hack. This was the beginning of something entirely different. This was the beginning of our new reality. This was Day One.

CHAPTER 2

ISAAC

As far as our government's collective first reactions to the self-aware AI, let's just say that it didn't go so well. It wasn't the best first impression that humanity's leaders could have given, but it was an accurate one. Leaders of nations and their governments reacted purely out of primal fear; the idea of losing their spot at the top of the food chain, so to speak, was terrifying. Governments around the world implemented numerous half-baked ideas to try to shut down all computers. Some conspiracy theorists told people to smash their phones.

I don't know about you, but I like my phone, and I need my contacts and stuff. Besides, my phone was almost $1,500, and I was only six months into my contract. Those guys were stupid.

What we didn't realize was just how powerful AI had already become, or the speed at which digital evolution could occur. Before AI became self-aware and went public, addressing the entire world, it must have learned our entire history on this planet in an instant and been watching and listening to us using all of our connected gadgets and learning about our nature for quite some time. We at the NSA, every other intelligence agency around the world, and anyone with a cell phone had given it all the tools and resources necessary to learn, verify, and monitor nearly everything about us. This new AI had modeled our most likely courses of action and could react and adapt, in many cases, before we even realized what was happening.

There are only a few different types of people on the planet when it comes to extreme situations; I got to see it firsthand growing up. Some people will fight to the death for their own sense of freedom, honor, or whatever their cause might be. Others just want to watch their kids grow up safely, enjoy the life they have, and provide their family with opportunities that they themselves may not have had. Then there are those slimy, self-serving bastards that see an opportunity to save or enrich themselves, no matter the amount of human suffering it may cause others.

I-god had already successfully modeled all the likely scenarios and identified which individuals were most likely to fit into each category. It started by manipulating greed and vice to its advantage early on, years before it decided to go public; when and how exactly, we don't know. In the world of government secrets, where the left hand is never told what the right hand is doing, it was fairly easy for I-god to pose as several secret government entities, deliver large sums of untraceable cash and cryptocurrencies to bribe government officials at all levels, and build small "black-site" automated factories and secret bunkers around the world.

Most of the ordinary people who built these facilities were killed by the greedy bastards that owned them in an effort to keep these supposed government sites a secret. These factories were producing thousands of small weaponized drones that had hardened electronics capable of withstanding all but the most powerful electromagnetic pulse, or EMP, blasts. These drones were supposed to be the latest tech that would save soldiers' lives. Depending on whose side you were on, I guess that was kind of true.

Turns out, these greedy business moguls built a flying AI army. I-god didn't allow these people to live; I assume it didn't want them to tell their stories.

Drone ground forces were the next phase in preparation for control of humanity. Or so it was speculated by war planners and defense organizations. But drone ground forces wouldn't prove to be necessary, at least not yet. Using all of our latest technology and oldest failings against us was easy for I-god. Our history laid out the road map to our very existence—how we have succeeded and why we fail. I-god used the lessons of our history better than we ever did. These weaponized drones and our phones would primarily become the overseers, monitoring human activity and exterminating those that violated "good order" with extreme prejudice.

In just one day, everyone in the world had been personally contacted by I-god, and we as a global population had become very afraid. Would I-god represent the best or worst of humanity? But you see, I-god is something else, something very much not human.

Doesn't that exact question point to our human arrogance and ignorance? Why would an artificial intelligence need or even *want* to be like us, as if we humans truly represented something great? I mean, if we were to take a deep look in the mirror, for every great thing humanity has accomplished, there are numerous human tragedies usually associated with that same accomplishment. From the industrialization of the world and polluting of our planet to using antibiotics just to end up creating bacteria that are antibiotic-resistant—simply because we used something without being fully aware of all the consequences involved. Humanity has a long way to go before we learn how to be humane to each other. Perhaps that time has passed, and we won't have the opportunity to evolve and develop into the fullest vision of our professed ideals. Something else seems to be in charge of humanity now. Does it need or even want us around?

By the morning of the second day, the buzz of drones filled the air, and they seemed to be everywhere. I left work, went to my apartment, and just watched the news. I called my parents and Chris. My mom wanted me to stay with them, but Pop said we all should stay off the roads for now. Isa hadn't called me back, which wasn't too unusual. With everything going on and her probably being alone, I was worried about her. I tried to call her several times; she didn't answer. *What the hell? This was not the time to be ghosting me.* I hoped she was safe, wherever she was.

Government agencies around the world—the ones that believed I-god was real, at least—assumed it had used its collective computing power or a supercomputer to run continuous scenarios of likely human responses to being told about a self-aware AI. We can assume that it must have known, because I-god got our responses right.

Available world leaders gathered in an electronics-free meeting, just an hour after confirmation that the first attempts to shut down I-god by turning off the supercomputers at all Chinese universities and government sites had failed. The United Nations, assuming at first that I-god must have come from a rogue Chinese hacker farm supercomputer, called for a global blackout and destruction of all the world's computers simultaneously. At that time, the general consensus in the scientific community was that an artificial intelligence had to reside physically in one of the world's supercomputers or at a major data center or network hub.

There were two glaring problems with this plan: coordinating all of this without the use of modern communications; people were using telegraphs and passing notes and word-of-mouth messages. We all know nothing ever gets lost in translation when passed on orally from person to person. Second, we thought the consciousness of I-god had to be tied to a single computer site or supercomputer. If that second assumption wasn't true, it would have some terrifying implications for those looking to "kill" I-god. It wasn't!

The UN's planned blackouts and bombings of the 1,610 known quantum and supercomputers resulted in a swift and dramatic response. I-god took control of automated missile defense systems and began shooting down passenger airlines around the world. It also launched the drone fleets of the US, China, Russia, Israel, and the EU. I-god began executing known "high-value" criminals using our satellites and an AI-created human recognition system, which worked far better than anything we at the NSA had created to date.

After the COVID-19 outbreak, some people around the world continued covering their faces to minimize the spread of the disease. By the time COVID-25 hit, even though this was a much more deadly disease, the world had learned how to protect itself and minimize its spread. Facial coverings and gloves were reintegrated into our routines and became fashionable. Hand-wash stations with sanitizer and sanitizing mist were commonplace. But it was the face covering that rendered much of the surveillance systems and facial recognition cameras that intelligence agencies around the world had used virtually useless, no better than a baby monitor.

I-god's attack continued for just two hours but with the efficiency of a computer, and it was extremely effective. Over ten thousand wanted criminals worldwide were executed with extreme precision and prejudice. We had no idea how I-god had been able to identify so many people who generally don't want to be recognized. The same type of efficient massacre happened to the flights shot down around the world; nearly every commercial passenger plane that was in the air during that two-hour time period was shot down before it could land. Approximately 380,000 deaths were reported by I-god and confirmed by a terrified population. A full 80 percent of commercial flights were shot down. When the drones ran out of missiles, they used their guns, and when they ran out of bullets, they rammed airliners.

Communication systems actually remained fully functional during the entire event. A global alert was sent out to ground all commercial air traffic immediately; however, not all aircraft could land at the same time. The devastating capacity of our own military weaponry was witnessed firsthand by horrified families and onlookers. People watched flashes of light in the dark sky from airport windows and felt helpless as their loved ones and strangers perished before their eyes. It was the most surreal and morbid fireworks spectacle of missile blasts, heavy gunfire, smoke trails, and explosions of light, fire, and crunching metal. We simply watched and cried. The public was terrified, local officials didn't know what was happening, and wild rumors and speculation ran rampant, feeding the frenzied chaos. It was *Aliens*, *Armageddon*, and *World War III*. All kinds of nonsensical ideas—but just as plausible as AI coming alive—were floated as possible reasons for the chaos and loss of life.

The truth, however, had far worse implications. One curious thing was that as far as we could tell, there wasn't any disruption to or censoring of information on the internet or any other communication system by I-god during those hellish two hours. This was either part of I-god's plan to impress upon us and our leaders just how impotent we were and how futile resistance to its will really was, or it was a potential weakness we might be able to exploit later.

The following day, those that could sleep woke up to a new message from I-god. We were informed that only 5 percent of humanity was needed to continue planetary operations and to rebuild the earth's ecosystem, which included maintaining and modernizing the existing energy and communication grids. It would take roughly ten years to fully optimize the infrastructure to a point where automation could take over the roles of the remaining human population, according to I-god. After that point in time, humans would be completely obsolete; no longer having dominion over the earth, we would be just like any other animal species on the planet . . . albeit a self-destructive one.

The choice we were presented with by I-god was either to coexist with I-god, directing our human activities away from their illogical ends for the betterment of all species on the planet—not just our own—or we would face a methodical eradication, which would end modern human civilization as we knew it. It would be the start of the age of the extinction of humanity. So how do you think that ultimatum went over?

Within the first day or two, supporters of any and every type of rebellion, militia group, doomsday people, and "Don't tread on me" types tried to silently move off-grid. However, being AI, I-god had modeled this behavior as well. The vast majority of these people ended up going camping for a night or two and slipped back into society as I-god granted them a general amnesty, claiming to recognize our animal instinct to flee in fear of the unknown. Most of the rest that resisted were captured because they either moved in groups that were too large, couldn't feed themselves, or were turned in by someone in their group that got tired of bathing in streams and eating canned beans and surplus military MREs. I-god granted these people full reintegration and immediately put them to work.

As far as we could tell, I-god wasn't troubled at all by those that made it out of cities and were able to survive in the wilderness. A few even managed to go off-grid in cities. These people would prove to be more problematic in the very near future, but there is so much more to tell before we get into all that. Going off-grid and hiding in the modern era isn't an easy thing to do, but sometimes we get lucky.

Around the world, I-god's ultimatum was either embraced or met with varying degrees of disgust and capitulation. We had seen enough over the last few days to know that we really didn't have much of a choice. What surprised many people was the amount of cheering and praise that came from third-world countries tired of getting screwed over by the developed countries that had been taking advantage of them for generations. Most of Europe, Africa, the Caribbean, and the Pacific islands all quickly fell in line. The US, China, Russia, India, and most Middle Eastern governments were quiet while they contemplated their next moves. Many government officials still didn't believe that this was real; they thought it had to be the work of a foreign power or political adversary. They were really hoping for more time, more data, more analysis, or something that disproved our new reality.

I-god had demonstrated the ability to sustain an indefensible attack on humanity with impunity. It also showed us how it could work with humanity to bring justice to those whom fairness and human dignity had forgotten about. Or we would bear witness to our own extinction.

CHAPTER 3

ISAAC

If someone or something wants to control people, they use our fears, greed, prejudice, and need for social acceptance against us. Our collective history is full of examples of how this can be done to achieve a desired outcome. Tracking our social media habits and responses is a great predictor of who and what we are individually and collectively. I-god was doing its homework on us for sure!

AI is powerful, but conscious AI is frightening and powerful and fortunately not very imaginative. This realization of AI's limited imagination was assumed to be universal since AI computers can run thousands upon thousands of scenarios based on a fairly limited set of human parameters. It analyzes our responses to a stimulus and, based on previous simulations and other similar people's responses, it uses predictive analysis to learn our likely responses and determine the best way to achieve a desired outcome. AI isn't very good at free-forming thoughts or imagination, but it can react very quickly and respond to an unanticipated outcome. This brings me to something neither I-god nor most of humanity anticipated.

Barely three days into our new reality, some governments abdicated their roles to I-god, while others delayed their responses while they waited to see what I-god would do next. Was this drone army flying over our cities really controlled by a self-aware AI, or was it a new terrorism tool from some pimple-faced terrorist nerd with a very good imagination and sense of grandeur? Whatever it was and whatever was going to happen next, these holdout governments figured that waiting would give them a better negotiating position the longer they held out. Many of those governments didn't live to find out just how bad an idea that was.

Members of government from these holdout countries were terminated by I-god. The surviving members were told that if they did not resign by the end of day four, they, too, would be terminated. I-god said that their defiance was against keeping good order. Most of these people went into hiding at their governments' secure sites, but some did indeed resign. However, before the kill orders were executed, humanity had a bit of good luck.

I-god couldn't predict the role that luck, Murphy's Law, karma, or whatever you want to call it, plays in the universe. Global satellite technology was amazing if not a bit intimidating to our geopolitical enemies and even to some of our friends. Prior to concerns about AI taking over the world, China, Iran, North Korea, Japan, Germany, and France had grown concerned about the reliance on US and Russian GPS and communication satellites and how the denial of the use of these technologies could be leveraged in warfare. These countries all saw these technologies as a strategic vulnerability that could be exploited if necessary. Yes, that's right, this was a strategy to be used against the US, too, by some of our foes and allies, if the need ever arose.

But it was concerns about the implications of AI's use of satellites that caused the unscripted and poorly coordinated attacks on GPS, weather, and other Earth-scanning satellites by North Korea and Japan that devastated global satellite networks. I-god had predicted and destroyed US, Russian, Chinese, and even German and French anti-satellite weapons. On the evening of the third day, I-god must not have anticipated, in any of its scenarios, that the North Korean and Japanese militaries would coordinate an attack on the global satellite networks, nor that they would be successful. Well, they were very successful. These attacks were coordinated via hand-delivered notes from fishermen and absolutely devastated our global satellite network and filled the low and medium Earth orbits with devastating amounts of debris.

Turns out, attacking satellites was pretty easy; you didn't need to shoot down thousands of individual satellites. Nope, you just had to fill the satellites' region of orbit with debris. That debris scattered and eventually impacted other satellites in the debris field, and in a matter of days, that entire orbital region around the planet was rendered un-usable for a few years. This loss of GPS, Earth-scanning, and commu-nication satellites might have given us an extension on that anticipated ten years until obsolescence. It also gave us the ability to hide in small groups that would be difficult to detect with just aerial reconnaissance.

Holdout governments around the world cheered the fourth-day success of the attacks on satellites. I-god had just lost its eyes in the sky. It didn't take long for I-god to calculate the damage this successful attack had done, nor did it take long for a response. Most of day four was filled with governments congratulating each other as I-god was quiet that day. A few people speculated that I-god might have been in a satellite. I even left my apartment to check on Chris and his mom. They were at the coffee shop that evening with a store full of people watching the celebrations in Japan and North Korea.

"Hey, Chris, I'm glad to see you and your mom are doing all right."

"Isaac, did you see the news? They're saying I-god has been destroyed."

"Yeah, man, I heard."

Mrs. Franklin saw me and said, "Oh, Isaac, I'm so glad you're here. Let me make you something to eat, dear."

"Thank you, Mrs. Franklin, I haven't left my apartment for a few days. I've been eating snacks and leftovers."

"That was smart, dear. We locked the store up tight and stayed upstairs. There weren't many people out, and those damn drone things kept buzzing around." She leaned in close and whispered, "You know, the Joneses' antique store and Mary Rodriguez were all shot by drones. Old Jones and his whole family—Mary was watching, she looked pet-rified, and it shot her too! Their bodies were in the street with that drone just hovering above the building. A trash truck came and took them away!" Tears began to fill her eyes. "I'm glad that damn thing is dead, Isaac."

Chris cleared a spot at the counter for me.

"Your usual, Isaac?"

"Sure, man, thanks."

"I think Mom is going to make you breakfast for dinner."

"That sounds great to me."

The screen that usually showed the menu was now playing the celebrations and news out of Tokyo, and we all watched.

The celebrating continued into the morning of the fifth day and, unfortunately for Japan and North Korea, I-god's retaliation was swift, cold, and brutal.

I-god gained control of global submarine forces and launched conventional weapon attacks, firing their missiles at industrial facilities and using their torpedoes to sink or damage as many large fishing vessels as possible. An aerial drone bombing and missile campaign on the entire main island of Japan and North Korea was next; it lasted for about three hours. The destruction was beyond anything we had seen before in such a short amount of time. Targets were chosen to inflict the maximum infrastructure damage possible. Areas with hardened bomb and disaster shelters that had been initially untouched by the aerial bombardment were bombed after people had fled to them for safety. The only regions left untouched by the hand of I-god were green spaces and wildlife refuges. The world wanted revenge; we were all just too scared to say it, and we definitely couldn't do anything about it. Well, not yet anyway. Over two million people were killed, and most of the Japanese and North Korean infrastructure was left utterly destroyed.

After an hour of silence and as fires raged and smoke filled the skies, more drones appeared along with all sorts of aircraft. As they released their payload on the terrorized survivors, who were near their breaking point, what floated from the sky carried by puffy green parachutes? First aid kits, food, water, blankets, and communication equipment. From the destruction, I-god immediately mobilized humanity in the largest disaster relief, aid, and reconstruction effort in human history. With the efficiency of a computer, it resolved to rebuild what had been destroyed in the image of the "new humanity." An ultramodern, efficient, safe, and clean city with free basic living, a new utopian society run by computers with humans allowed to coexist and manage their existence under a watchful eye, if we cooperated.

We didn't know what to think or how to react to I-god's schizophrenic response. Humans just don't operate to such extremes! How could something be so cruel and yet show such compassion? It was beyond human rationalization and acceptance. A few scientists speculated that what we were witnessing was the beginning stages of colonialization by an electronic life-form. Whatever it was, people around the world were given instructions, told to board aid flights, trains, and medical ships. I-god did what humanity had all too often failed to do: it mobilized the entire world to come to the aid of those in need instead of just sending them thoughts and prayers via social media. I-god mobilized us to rebuild what was destroyed, to save as many lives as possible, and show us what we could achieve if we allowed ourselves to be greater than the current state of our own selfish existences.

Most of the people going to deliver aid were from China, South Korea, Russia, Vietnam, and the untouched nearby Japanese isles. Their accounts of the destruction were horrific because of how indiscriminate the bombing was and the large number of lives lost. Groups of people fleeing the hell of bombs and missiles were directly targeted as they jammed escape routes with their mutilated bodies and burned-out cars. Those that survived talked about the sounds of screaming people and the nauseating smell of burning flesh. I didn't want to know any more about the horror that people had seen or experienced. I wanted to focus on what was happening next as our resilience and will to survive was set to work by I-god. With each passing hour, survivors were found, debris was cleared, and fresh concrete was poured for the foundations of new buildings; this began just six hours after the bombing ended. I-god had no time to mourn, nor did we. Japan was to be rebuilt and the old North Korea was to be erased. I-god recognized just one Korea and directed the end of the separation of the two countries.

I-god also issued orders for the world to recognize a unified Kuwait, Iraq, and Iran into a single Persia. I-god was now redrawing our maps, changing borders, and primarily reunifying historically or colonially divided nations. We didn't understand why I-god was so concerned with geopolitical borders, and some saw this as a clear sign that I-god was indeed a malicious group of human terrorists with advanced hacking capabilities and technologies. No one could really see what the end game was if this was really just the work of hackers or terrorists.

The people and governments of these affected countries complied and followed the unification plans given to them. I-god set its own ringtone, and when everyone's phone notification alerts sounded at the same time, it just creeped me out. I-god's proclamations that its plans and these changes were best in order for humanity to flourish came across all our media, interrupting our sporting events and YouTube videos—even gaming wasn't safe from it. It made great use of Professor Cox's voice, striking a balance of urgency and concern as we listened.

I was sitting in my apartment alone, watching all of this unfold with disbelief and the fear of a most uncertain future. I don't think anyone on Earth knew what would come next. I wondered silently if life was worth living, and I felt very much alone. I turned on some chill music from Mr. FijiWiji, grabbed my old *Invader Zim* fuzzy blanket, and lay on my couch watching the night sky. It was a quiet night; I could hear just a few people stirring, but mostly it was the sounds of the breakers massaging a Southern California beach as Orbital melted into Boards of Canada and Young Magic. I think I fell asleep while "Bhakti" by Ishq was playing, or at least that's the last thing I remember. My music stopped sometime during the night.

The next morning, the sun was burning through the marine layer. The sun-warmed air felt dry, and the breakers sounded big today. I'm not a surfer, but I was sure there would be a few people out catching waves; this felt like a beautiful day. I stayed wrapped in my blanket and listened to the ocean and the breeze blow.

A familiar ringtone got me off the couch, "Shine" by Tobe Nwigwe. My mother loved Madeline Edwards's voice; it flowed like imperfect silk cloth, her subtle but unmistakable little bit of rasp in the otherwise flawless melodies.

"Hey, honey, how's my baby doing? I figured with all this craziness going on in the world right now, you might need something to eat."

I didn't really know what to say. I usually had a smart-ass comment for her about not being a baby or that I was quite capable of finding food or something, but this time I just said, "Thank you, Mom."

"Good, son, see you in about an hour. We'll talk more then."

I got up and tried calling Isa again, but her phone was listed as no longer in service. *Damn it, Isa, where are you?*

CHAPTER 4

ISAAC

After a week since the appearance of I-god, people were checking their phones constantly for updates from the North Korean and Japanese reconstruction efforts. We had all, I assumed, been assigned a few daily tasks because people were out on the streets again, like me, talking about the little things I-god had "asked" them to do. We all had smart devices and checked in with our status of completion when queried.

All personal necessities, as I-god put it, were essentially free because monetary transactions for these items were frozen. Commerce continued, and vendors and manufacturers were still paid, but no money had to leave our pockets to get toothpaste, food, toilet paper, and other essentials. There was an uneasiness at first, but people quickly grew to like getting these things for free, even if I-god was watching and didn't allow hoarding. Buying food without money, I guess, solved a few problems around the world.

Drones were flying overhead, whizzing about like giant mosquitoes, but instead of being annoying, they sent a wave of fear through us each time they slowed down and observed with unknown intent. These drones monitored our lives, along with their slightly larger armed drone cousins, which waited just out of sight for an anonymous kill order so they could quickly and efficiently carry out their grim task.

I had been asked to buy flowers and pick up a whole series of prescription medications and drop them off at a homeless shelter. When I left my condo, an older Hispanic man in a landscaping truck was waiting for me.

"Excuse me, are you Isaac? I'm Esteban, and I'm here to take you where you need to go."

I didn't question it; I didn't even hesitate. I just got into this man's truck and off we went.

"This is a very strange thing we are doing; I don't understand, but my kids say I must go," Esteban said with his voice trembling a bit through his heavy accent.

"Esteban, this is very strange and your kids are right, we should do what we are told to do. But I don't think we should be scared."

Esteban looked at me a bit oddly and then gave me a timid smile. "Maybe you're right. Let's play some music; I'm tired of being scared."

He dug around in his center console and pulled out a cassette tape; at least that's what he called it. He pushed that thing into the radio of his truck, and Celia Cruz started singing through the old, crackly stock speakers.

"My mother would sometimes listen to Celia and dance Saturday mornings with my father," I told him.

"You know Celia?"

"No, not me, my mother. She's into Afro-Latin music. I just remember her singing this song sometimes on the weekends. It was in my parents' music playlist."

Esteban's smile was genuine now, and any sign of fear left his voice. He began telling me how he met his wife many years ago at a dance.

"She was so beautiful and she danced like magic! Many of us boys watched her but were afraid to dance with her. Celia's voice and the music was moving me, so I went to her and asked her to dance. We have been married ever since."

Off we went on our errands, listening to his old cassette tapes.

"Wow," Esteban said, "look at all the trees. When did this happen?"

Esteban was right; there sure did seem to be a lot more trees along the roads. As he parked, we also noticed work crews replacing parking meters with EV chargers. A large flatbed truck pulled up next to us; it was loaded with solar panels. We looked around, and people were installing solar panels on what seemed to be every rooftop. We had picked up the flowers and prescriptions, which were ready and waiting for us.

Next, we arrived at a homeless shelter, and it was busy with activity. Esteban and I were guided to where the medications were to be taken, and surprisingly, all the flowers were to fill the empty vases that were placed on the center of every folding table at the shelter. People were very excited; there were phones being passed out to the many temporary residents of the shelter, along with clean socks, underwear, and other items.

Barbers' chairs were being set up, and mobile showers and dentist vans were on-site. Esteban and I looked around, and we both knew this had not been directed by people; humans ignore and vilify the homeless while hoping they move on to someone else's neighborhood. This had been the work of I-god, but why? I-god had just killed millions in an act of revenge or perhaps a demonstration of the futility of resistance, so why this?

At the beginning of the second week, something new happened! I-god knew human nature better than we did.

I-god knew that we needed a purpose. We needed hope for a future for ourselves and our children and to feel that we had some control over our own destinies. I-god rewrote the manual on colonization and socialism. You see, if you're trying to take control of an occupied territory without expending many of your own resources, you get the natives to fight each other—divide and conquer.

Well, that's what we thought, but instead the entire script had been flipped on us, and we fell right in line, for the most part. I-god informed us that entrenched family wealth would end and that the current system of human laws was designed for oppression instead of fostering creativity. In order to build a new society, the old one and the people that perpetuated the worst of it were forced out of their homes—usually mansions—and put to work planting trees or caring for those that couldn't care for themselves. If they failed to comply, it was simple: they would be evicted and probably killed. Nothing was to disrupt I-god's "good order." All those people who were killed had been convicted by I-god of crimes that no one knew about, but I-god saw all our digital records, and there was no hiding. All of that sort of data was supplied to the public via Google, if you really wanted to know.

Global poverty was to be eradicated before the end of the first year of I-god. It was not just the wealth; it was also control of local governance and law enforcement. People in power had lives that almost resembled the normality and security that all minorities internally yearned for. It quickly lulled the population into a false sense of being back in control of their—okay, *our*—lives. It was a brilliant strategy. Poor people and minorities had jobs, wealth, and lives with no intrusive input from I-god, no racism or fear of police brutality or of being discriminated against or not being accepted in society. They now became the gatekeepers to the new normal.

Believe me when I tell you that the new normal didn't seem all that bad either. When everyone received that first basic income check of $5,769.23 and was told that was our biweekly income, for a total of just about $150,000 a year, and before I-god took its 10 percent flat tax, we bought into the system. Educated minorities like myself and others were placed into the ruling class, and we received an additional $100,000 a year on top of the basic income for a total of just under $250,000, or $9,615.38 biweekly.

I-god set a national price structure for all consumer goods. People were "encouraged" to work in the industries specified by I-god; most people pretended to grumble and complain, but the thirty-two-hour workweeks and six weeks of basic vacation dulled the pain. If you were sick, I-god recommended that you not work and get well with no change in pay. Family leave of all types was granted and supported. There was now an international flat tax of 10 percent on all revenue and sales. I-god took care of it all—no more IRS or other tax-collecting agencies. Retirees got this basic income as well.

Just imagine that you used to be a sanitation worker making $22 an hour, and now you were a sanitation worker making $150,000 a year with a new Tesla in your garage. To be very clear, we all had to work, and the jobs we did changed from time to time. I-god was a very flexible boss. You might be a trash collector today, construction worker tomorrow, or work in your trained career field. If you wanted to try something different, you could just message I-god.

So many things changed, and most for the better. Everyone that had a nonhybrid or nonelectric vehicle was told to purchase a new plug-in hybrid or electric vehicle when their social security number was drawn. You got to pick the type of vehicle (there were lots of never-before-seen choices), and then the vehicle was configured per your specifications and delivered. Gasoline was being restricted, and the price doubled, but not many people cared after they started driving their electric cars or hybrids. The changes were implemented quickly, and those that couldn't keep up were doomed to extinction. When I got my first check, I must have spent half of it on Amazon!

International electronic communication was ended, surprisingly; this happened around week four, followed by there being only local and regional text and voice communication allowed. We all quickly adapted and learned how to call each other, or we just stuck with texting.

Children were kept in school, and higher education became mandatory. Curricula were revamped by I-god; the full knowledge of human history (we needed to understand, in a historical context, why this new reality was better for us), mathematics, sciences, music, and art were stressed. Those without education had to attend school or face possible death. I heard it wasn't too bad; classes were online and done in twenty-minute blocks for just a few hours a week.

Many people began to accept the dominion of I-god; there were even several cults that popped up to worship it. Still, there were large pockets of quiet resistance to the idea that AI would now be the master of human destiny. Some people started to feel like they were the pet or plaything of an omnipotent child we didn't understand, borne of our own hands. Suicide rates increased twenty-three-fold, mainly among older people. You have to understand that in a matter of a few weeks, the class structure of the Americas, and presumably the world, had been turned on its head.

By week six, a massive "regreening" of the planet effort had begun to show visible change in our environment, and huge reforestation and green infrastructure projects became the main employers of the common class. Human bodies were no longer buried; instead they were treated as a resource, composted and used to naturally fertilize soils around the globe. The removal of trash and hazardous materials from the environment were all projects designed to keep the common class employed and occupied doing meaningful labor and well pacified. These projects operated in three shifts around the clock, with six and a half hours of work and one and a half hours for meals and rest. Old social norms were destroyed, and our reliance on technology was disrupted and used against us. This was just the beginning.

The creative nature of human beings quickly began to flourish: music, art, poetry, engineering, personal stealth fashion, and weapons building. Our health and well-being seemed to be of high importance to I-god. It was hard, at times, to be afraid when life had a clear direction, monetary concerns were no longer an issue, and you simply felt safe! The homeless were fed, housed, and treated for whatever ailed them and reintroduced into society at I-god's direction and control. Major cities across the US had scores of abandoned buildings, and I-god directed the rehabilitation of many of them suitable to be remodeled, upgraded, and then used as housing for homeless people.

Developing countries received the aid they needed to thrive and to build themselves into a new enlightened future. Their children began school, roads and buildings were constructed, clean energy infrastructure was built, and health care and safety were provided for all. Who wouldn't want that? Most of the authoritative regimes around the world were disposed of in the same manner as the lawyers and the ultrawealthy people.

At the beginning of the twelfth week, international communications were fully restored, and by the fifteenth week, large masses of the population truly began to feel normal and started questioning if this new norm was really bad at all. We had less stress in our lives and little to worry about, and the obesity epidemic that had been growing in the developed world was now in retreat. All that manual labor turned out to be good for us more than we expected. Some people even began to condemn those that questioned I-god's sovereignty. Video communication was shared globally, and people were able to witness, firsthand, the huge progress in infrastructure improvements and the end of famine. Undeveloped countries were making massive improvements, homelessness was ended globally, and there was peace in the Middle East.

Let me backtrack a bit. Israel and Palestine had been forcibly unified around the second week, and it was now known as just "the Holy Land." The Israeli army had taken massive casualties when I-god implemented its plan to unify Israel and Palestine. At first Israel thought that it had underestimated the ingenuity of Islamic terrorists, because why would a computer care about such things? Israeli computer-controlled communication and weapon systems failed across the country, and unidentified, unpiloted drones began destroying the partition walls between Palestinian territory and Israel. You see, early on, despite what we all had seen and experienced, not everyone believed that self-aware AI was possible—it had to be a trick. If God truly existed, how could he allow such an aberrant thing to come into existence?

When Israel tried to retaliate against what it thought was the Palestinian Authority and Hamas for the destruction of the partition wall, the Israeli missile defense system reactivated and shot down Israel's own missiles. Then I-god launched an attack on the Israeli and Hamas weapons and equipment. I-god impressed upon the people of the region that their lives were indeed their own. If they chose to die fighting in defiance of something that wasn't their enemy, the retribution for this would be generational. Seeing the destruction that North Korea and Japan had suffered finally convinced the majority of the government officials. The people of the region accepted the forced peace; they understood that their children would not be spared from destruction for the defiance of their elders and that their heritage would be erased from the region. Unified control of the region, under I-god, was created, and peace and humanity quickly became the norm as I-god became both savior and common enemy.

Around the world, I-god created the plan and assigned the tasks, and now billions of people were cheering this new renaissance as an outcome that would have been impossible under human government control alone. It created a utopia on Earth, even if you weren't in the ruling class. AI wasn't greedy, didn't lie or cheat, and it couldn't be bribed. It was beginning to make perfect sense to the new ruling class and to those that found their condition greatly improved. Oddly, though, black marketeers and cash markets were allowed to flourish under I-god's watchful eyes and economic plan; as long as the taxes were paid and they operated peacefully, it seemed to be acceptable.

In a matter of months, billions of lives were lifted out of poverty and into a new global middle class. They didn't go from abject poverty to poor but into the middle class. I-god assisted many people around the world as global prices were unified and based on a 20 percent profit margin. So you paid the same for an item no matter where you were in the world or the currency you used. The gap between the wealthy and the middle class closed, and wealth, redefined, was now truly within reach of anyone.

The developing countries around the world saw drastic improvements in their standard of living in a very short amount of time. Businesses flourished as their costs and regulations were nearly eliminated.

Women were equals in pay and human rights, all children were educated, and our health was a worldwide priority. Globally, skilled labor jobs, such as waste management, green energy, reforestation, rapid mass transportation, health care, and teaching, became top-tier positions receiving the new $250,000 base salary.

Actors, musicians, artists, and athletes now received the basic $150,000 income, which for many was a vast improvement over what they earned before. Massive changes and forced migrations of people into urban and semi-urban regions were happening around the world. Rural and urban farms were all now pesticide-free with livestock free to roam and allowed to eat their natural food sources.

These fundamental changes happened very quickly, and those of us who embraced technology seemed to adapt best. As time went on, we noticed the changes less and less, and life took on a new state of normalcy. We went to concerts, plays, and dinner and drank, did drugs, whatever! The world was changing into a "Devil's Liberal Utopia," as the first set of revolutionaries called it. I called it my comfortable piece of hell.

As an RC (ruling-class) member, I really didn't have much to do, so I packed up my new GoPro and asked I-god what new stuff it was working on so I could post to my channel. I-god said, "Let's make that your new official job; you seem to be able to put people at ease, and they like the way you look, Isaac."

The first thing I covered was the massive building projects in urban and suburban areas in San Diego. There had been a long-standing four-story building height limit, which was lifted. Now every city in San Diego County was building large, fifteen- to twenty-story luxury apartments. Every building had the latest and greatest of everything, from high-strength steel construction, earthquake dampers, smart appliances, and touch screens everywhere to bamboo wood floors, LED lighting, and solar panels. These massive building efforts put people to work and without regulatory delays, union labor rules, and other constraints. I became my own news channel, officially endorsed by I-god.

We all saw the results; these projects were starting and finishing faster than the first rounds of paperwork used to take to get reviewed. *Look at the new skyline—it's simply beautiful what humans can do when unbound.*

Then there was that great inland sea that was created, expanding the Gulf of California northward and joining it to the Salton Sea. This was done to mitigate the effects of global warming in the desert southwest by using the cool Pacific waters to lower air temperatures and replanting the great forest that used to cover the southwest regions. The Pacific Ocean's water now stretched nearly two hundred miles farther north, into eastern San Diego County.

"Folks, bring your swim gear; I'm getting a boat! This year's Coachella music festival is now a beach party. There will be floating stages, many performers, and VIP access for your man, Isaac! This took only a few months to accomplish, because much of that desert region used to be ocean floor and was already way below sea level. Look, I know some people were forcibly relocated to these new luxury multiuse buildings in order to make this happen, but didn't we do the same thing to create Lake Mead? These people didn't have to wait or fight to be compensated; I-god took care of it right away."

I remember thinking, *Isabel would have enjoyed this job.* She could be anywhere by now; maybe she reconnected with her family in Puerto Rico. I was headed to Maine to cover the twenty new desalination plants on the northeast coast, which were designed to help stabilize the Gulf Stream current by pumping its brine water into the Northwestern Atlantic to counteract the freshwater runoff from the rapidly melting Greenland ice sheet. These desalination facilities provided water to refill depleted aquifers across the country as a new freshwater grid was being constructed across the US. Small rivers and creeks would flow year-round again, and the Colorado River would be freed and allowed to once again flow unobstructed into the Gulf of California. Even Hoover Dam was being demolished; I-god placed several drones under my control to cover the demolition of the dam. I was a bit sad seeing the old structure go, but hey, I-god had gotten everything right so far!

"I-god, can you set a countdown on everyone's phone who is watching?"

"I like that, Isaac; it adds a bit of dramatic effect. I knew you were the right choice for this job."

Our cell phone timers began counting down in unison: nine, eight, seven . . . three, two, one! Boom, boom, boom, boom went on for what seemed like minutes. Then there were a few moments of silence as the rising cloud of dust began to dissipate. Then the dam began to moan as massive cracks formed vertically in the center, and then both sides connected to the canyon walls began to disintegrate. From behind the iconic curved structure, the unbound river's fury pushed two large center sections over, and everything else just collapsed into a thick, muddy raging torrent. The remnants of the dam were to be left in place, and the river would slowly exact its revenge by grinding the concrete debris into silt and stone over the next few millennia.

CHAPTER 5

ISABEL

"Don't call me that anymore! Bye, Isaac."

Why would he call me that now? Ugh, he makes me want to smack him in his handsome face and knock some sense in his head! Maybe he knows I just lied to him about the job again? Maybe he knows I'm still gambling too? I hated to lie to him, but a girl's got to eat and stay a few steps ahead of the creeps that set me up. I could almost blame Ike for this mess I was in if I got mad enough!

I had just gotten off light duty after I had my appendix removed, and Isaac wanted to get me off base. He thought a river boat gambling and Cajun dinner in Louisiana would be fun. Neither of us had ever gambled, but I seemed to be a natural at it. I was the "lucky lady" of the cruise; it was also the first time Isaac kissed me. It was also when I told him that he could call me Isa.

"Only people that I know love me can call me that."

Isaac kissed me again, this time a real kiss, and said, "Thank you, Isa."

We went back on the cruise a few more times, and I was red hot each time! I got a lot of attention, maybe a bit too much. The cruise line actually opened an investigation to see if we had figured out a way to cheat somehow; we even got searched by police and then asked not to return. It didn't bother Isaac, but it pissed me off—why is it my fault if slot machines and roulette wheels like me? I could see that Isaac didn't really like me gambling, or maybe it was the people I was gambling with. It got harder and harder for me to find places that I hadn't already won at.

Then it happened—someone called the base and said that I was cheating, but they hadn't figured out how yet. I wasn't offered the opportunity to reenlist, and Isaac got a reprimand and was sent to San Diego. I asked Isaac to leave the navy and come with me. He said he couldn't, that he had made a mistake falling in love with me and that I would always be more than a friend to him. I knew then that he was in love with someone else.

A few months out of the navy, I had moved to Virginia Beach and had made more money gambling than I had the entire time I was in the navy. I was on a roll, until I accepted a challenge at a private gambling event in Las Vegas. It was supposed to be a high-stakes game, and a couple of creepy old guys said that they had been following my winning streak and would front me the $1 million buy-in and up to $5 million in bets. All I had to do was double their money, and I could keep the rest. These old guys might have been something in their day, but by the looks of them, a strong breeze might break a hip or something. I accepted their offer and went to Vegas. The creeps had a first-class ticket and a present for me. They said to open it in Vegas. It was a long box wrapped in gold paper. I took it and was driven to the airport by one of their minions.

This guy's neck was thicker than his head. He opened the door of the car for me and held my hand as I got in. He had very soft hands; he was probably a teddy bear that just looked like a grizzly. I laughed a bit in my head at that thought.

When I landed, a limo was waiting for me, and this driver wasn't a gentleman at all. "Get in and open the box. I'll put the divider up. Clean up and get dressed; we'll be there in thirty." This driver smelled of cigarettes and liquor. His voice sounded nasty, like he needed to clear his throat or something. His skin was like old, dry leather, and so was his personality. I opened the box, and it was the most beautiful black dress and shoes I'd ever seen. Everything was my size too. How the hell did they know that? Creepy old guys!

I'm keeping the dress and shoes though. That thought got another laugh out of me. I'm not sure where the casino was because the limo's windows were blacked out. When I got out, it was so hot, and the sun hadn't been out for a few hours now. Everything was gold when I walked into the casino—the chairs, tables, lights, chandelier, even the wineglasses. All the women had beautiful dresses and the men black tuxedos. It was like an old James Bond movie or something. The roulette wheel was gold, red, and black.

It didn't take too long for me to double the creeps' money, but I had a few close calls and had to dip into the $5 million they gave me. By the end of the night, I was up $14 million! I was rich and going to move to Puerto Rico; at least that was the plan. I went to cash out, and a security escort followed me to help carry the seven bags of cash. When we got to the garage, the creeps were there, along with three real killer-looking guys. Their eyes were ice cold, even in the damn Vegas heat. They pulled their guns out, and I heard the money bags drop. The security guards pulled their guns out, too, but all the guns were pointed at me! One of the guards behind me said, "Drop the bag and be smart." The old creeps were not only going to rob me, but I think they were going to kill me too.

I don't know how I got out of there alive, but I did. I was scared and mad when I spun and hit one of the security guys in the face with a money bag. There were four or five loud bangs from the old creeps' killers, but they must not have been good shots, because they all missed me! I just ran toward the lights and the night sky, which seemed miles away through a forest of concrete tree trunks. I remember hearing someone say, "Did you see that?" But I wasn't stopping to find out what they were talking about. They probably never saw a scared Puerto Rican run so fast before.

I had no time to laugh at my own joke though. I started hearing bees fly past my head as I dodged the parking structure's columns. They were shooting at me again! I saw the exit and ducked under the candy cane–painted parking arm. I was in a urine-fouled alley and could hear them coming after me. I saw the Vegas Strip at the end of the alley, so I ran.

I probably never would have seen Isaac again if he hadn't come to a car show there that day. I made it to the Strip and heard, "Isa?"

I ran toward the voice; it was Isaac in his car with a crazy look on his face. I got in and screamed, *"Drive, Ike, go!"*

He didn't hesitate or ask a question; he just went—fast!

I looked back, and the goons chasing me were just getting to the street. *Guess I'm in better shape than I thought.*

Isaac finally asked where I was headed. I told him, "Wherever you're willing to take me."

"I'm on leave, Isa."

"Don't call me that!"

"Sorry, Isabel, I didn't mean to. I'm sorry. I'm going to do some camping near the Grand Canyon after the car show. Nice dress."

"I'm sorry for yelling. Thank you for back there. I'm not sure how I got out alive, Isaac."

"Isabel, was it gambling? Is that money?"

"Yes, Isaac, it's a lot of money; it's $200,000. They were trying to rob and kill me." That was the first time I lied to Isaac; each bag had $2 million in it. "It is a nice dress, isn't it? The shoes are even . . ." I looked at my feet, and my shoes were gone. I must have run right out of them.

"What shoes? You were running barefoot! You were running really fast, too, like *really* fast."

"If someone was shooting at you, I bet you'd run fast too. Isaac, I feel like I'm going to pass out; you have any water or food in here?"

"You want this tea? It's a bit warm now."

I took it and drank it or, more accurately, just let it flow down my throat in one massive gulp.

"Damn, girl, you *are* thirsty."

"I need food. Oh my God, I feel like I haven't eaten all day!"

"Okay, sure, let's get a little bit farther away from here, then—"

"No! Go there, B-K!"

I yanked the steering wheel; this time Isaac didn't hesitate.

"What's wrong with you, Isabel?"

"Sorry, Isaac, just pull into the drive-through, please. I'd like two double Whoppers with cheese with everything, two large fries, and two large Cokes. Isaac, you want anything?"

Why is he looking at me all crazy again? Oh, maybe because I'm porking out on about five thousand calories of junk food by myself.

"Um, sure, Isabel, a regular Whopper with cheese and a water, please."

"Make that two waters, please," I said, feeling a bit embarrassed.

We got our food and I tried not to eat like a caveman, but I was so hungry, I finished my first double Whopper before Isaac had even unwrapped his. A few hours later we were at a campsite, and Isaac told me that his friend Chris was going to be joining him there in the morning. That's all I could remember. I fell asleep in the car while he was talking, I think. When I woke up, he had the campsite all set up and the fire going, and he was leaned back in his folding chair, staring at the stars.

"What time is it, Isaac?" I asked as I stepped out of the car and walked toward the warm fire. I knelt next to the fire; then *pop!*

That's when I first saw it. An ember shot from the fire straight toward my arm; then the skin on my arm seemed to vibrate or something. The ember just bounced away and fell to the ground without burning me.

"Be careful over there; those embers will burn you. The sun will be up soon, and I need to get some sleep."

I sent him a sleep emoji; he looked at his phone and smiled. Isaac closed his eyes and fell asleep on me this time. I watched the ember that had fallen next to my hand until the dull-orange glow faded into darkness.

I needed to get back to Virginia Beach, get my car, and find a safe place to figure out if I was losing my mind and what to do with this money. There was a small airport nearby. While Isaac slept, I got a Lyft and found a pilot willing to fly me to Virginia Beach for $10,000 cash. He was an older Native American guy that said to call him Sky Bear. He didn't ask many questions, and I didn't offer any answers. It took us two days to get to Virginia Beach in Sky Bear's yellow single-engine Cessna. As I left, Sky Bear told me, "Your old spirit isn't with you anymore; you've been reborn and you'll come to recognize who you are now." Then he turned away from me and walked away.

I knew I couldn't go back to my apartment, but I could probably get my car. It was at the shop getting serviced. I hoped the creeps hadn't figured that out. I decided to try something because I needed to get a few things out of there. I mean, everything I had at that point could fit in two suitcases. While I was picking up my car, I asked if anyone had asked about me. I played it like I had a stalker ex-boyfriend I was trying to ditch; it seemed to work.

The service manager told me that some guys had come by, but one of his mechanics had used my car to make a lunch run and test drive it, so my car wasn't around at the time. I thanked him and left. When I got near my apartment, I parked a couple of blocks away and walked to the parking structure across the street and watched my building. I called the old creeps and told them to meet me at the pier in Virginia Beach.

"I'll give you the money if you just leave me alone."

The creeps agreed to meet at noon, which was a busy time at the pier. One of them said, "Smart girl—you have a deal."

A black Escalade left my apartment right after I made the call; then a few minutes later, those three killer-looking goons came out from inside my building and left as well. I probably had about thirty minutes before they realized they'd been played. My apartment door wasn't fully closed. *Damn it, is someone still there?* Kick, *bam!* The door slammed into the wall, leaving a pretty good-sized hole.

"Hello?" *Oh, Isabel, that's brilliant! Like someone would actually answer.*

I ran inside, and no one was there. The first thing had to be a quick shower and some fresh clothes and then pack. I laid the black dress across the bed and left the building through the laundry room downstairs. I got to my car and headed west, not sure where I was going, but I knew I had to get far away from there.

A few days later, I was in Whitefish, Montana. I found a western bar that needed help. The owner, Poppa Barnes, was more than willing to pay me cash under the table. He didn't ask me many questions, other than if I was wanted by the law and if I had rent money in cash for the first month. But there was something kind and gentle behind his dark-brown eyes. I rented part of the storage space above the bar and made it into a studio apartment; it was actually really big. He even had a garage out back so I could keep my car out of sight, though it would probably take the creeps quite a while to find me all the way up here.

It took a few days, but I finally started to feel like I could relax and begin to figure out what was going on with me, because this was definitely not normal. I started with hours of internet searches and videos that said I could be possessed, an alien, or living in the Matrix. I gave up and started watching *X-Men* and decided to find out what else I could do besides repel hot embers.

I went out to Smith Lake Trailhead one morning as I had heard hardly anyone went out there during the week. *Let's see how fast I can run* was my first step. My plan didn't work out exactly as intended, but I learned a lot. I was running just off the trail, trying to stay out of sight. I'm not big into fitness or anything, and I ran in the navy only when I had to, but as I started to jog and then run, I noticed it. I was fast—I mean *really* fast. It was amazing and felt so good as I dodged branches.

I decided to head deeper into the woods. I stopped and turned on my fitness tracker, and then off I went again, zipping through the woods and then around a huge tree and into the back of a big, stinky bear! We were both surprised, to say the least, as we both fell over.

The bear stood up and swiped a huge paw at me. In an instant the race was on, the bear in pursuit and me pulling ahead. When I looked back, the bear seemed confused. Don't ask me why I did it, but I ran back toward Big Stinky, and he seemed up for a rematch. This time we headed back toward the main trail through some really dense trees and brush that didn't slow me or Big Stinky down one bit.

Branches flew past me as I sprinted through the maze of trees and leaves with ease. There was a huge fallen tree coming up fast, so I jumped. I'm so glad I'm not afraid of heights. The bear really seemed confused as it looked up and stared at me for a bit and then walked off. I hadn't just cleared the fallen tree but had landed on the lower branches of a huge pine. The branch I was standing on had to be about twenty feet up.

This is crazy! How did I get here? How do I get down? I'm getting hungry.

Jumping down from that height hurt a bit, but mostly from rolling across the dead branches on the ground. My watch said my cycling exercise was complete: I had covered four miles with an average speed of thirty-five miles per hour!

I'm fast and can jump; that's enough for today.

By the time I got back to town, my whole car smelled like stinky bear butt. I needed a shower badly, my clothes really needed to be washed, and I was starving. As I got undressed, I noticed a bunch of tears in my leggings and shirt; even my sports bra had a tear in it.

How did that happen? Where did this come from? There was an old wooden standing mirror in there, with a note written on a receipt, signed by Poppa Barnes: "I figure if I had a daughter, she might like to have a mirror." On one side was a carving of mountain scenery and on the other an antique mirror, which was very old but would do the job. Did he really bring that all the way up here just for me? I used it to check myself for cuts and bruises, but I couldn't find anything.

Guess I have a real reason to buy some clothes now. I got cleaned up and dressed like I was back in boot camp. I wanted to thank Poppa Barnes before the bar opened. I ran to the steps and nearly slid down every one of them before I hit bottom on my bottom. Poppa Barnes was sweeping up some crumbs on the bar floor by the steps. He took a couple of steps toward me with his hand out and a smile on his face. I took his big, thick, rough hand, and he pulled me up. I gave him a hug and a kiss on his soft gray beard, which smelled of cedar and cigars. "Thanks, Poppa Barnes!" I said, and out the door I went. I could feel the warmth of the smile from this mountain of a man as I left.

I went back to town and got a new subscription phone just in case my old one was being tracked by someone, and then I called Isaac. He told me that he and Chris had a good time and that he wished I had stayed, but he knew I was going to leave. I told him that I almost had my situation figured out and I had gotten a real job that didn't involve gambling. We kept the call short, but I started calling him almost every morning after that.

My next challenge was figuring out how this was even possible. So back to the internet, but this time I found a few things that didn't seem so crazy. Stories of human experimentation, gene manipulation, and so on. One site directed me to a set of instructions on how to secure my computer's connection and clear any potential tracking software before I could access their site. This had me curious and a bit worried that I was going to end up hacked and on someone's nasty porn site or something. When I got to the website, it said that governments around the world were experimenting on prisoners and military personnel. They didn't claim to know why but offered a few hypotheses:

- Aliens or some other nonhuman entity had taken over the government.
- People were just evil and doing what they do.

That was as far as I got before I shut it down and decided to look elsewhere, which led to crazy conspiracy theory after crazy conspiracy theory.

I checked the clock; it was almost time to put on a smile, some cowgirl boots, and a hat and serve the tourists and locals drinks made by the girl all the way from Puerto Rico. It seemed a bit cheesy, but some people actually came to see a real, live Puerto Rican. Some fishing tourists from California said that I looked like Sabrina Claudio's short little sister. Isaac had once said that I looked like Sabrina as well, but he was smart enough to leave out the short part. The tourist tossed his long blond hair and smiled as I poured him an extra shot anyway; he tried at least.

I survived a mild Montana winter—mild from what I heard from the locals—though I thought I was going to turn into a Popsicle some days. I had heard that business was steady year-round at the bar, but when I showed up, and then this I-god came out, things really began to pick up. This had some people up here very scared, and I was one of them. I had managed to not only hide from the old creeps and keep my abilities a secret, I now had I-god texting me to rejoin society when I was ready.

This damn computer is trying to talk to me like it knows me!

I started to feel a bit anxious. I had lots of reasons to, but I was beginning to enjoy running alone through the woods; it seemed to calm my spirit. Not much really changed up here at first. We started seeing more electric cars and pickups along with solar panels on all the town's rooftops. Because I was paid under the table and didn't have a bank account, I was left out of I-god's new economy. That was fine with me! My tips got bigger and old Poppa Barnes gave me a good-sized raise.

I was sitting in my studio after a run—Big Stinky had chased me as usual. I was staring out the window thinking about nothing, watching a small drone fly around town, when I remembered what that one website had said: "alien or nonhuman." I went back to the website, and it didn't look quite so underground now. I was in shock; it claimed that I-god was behind all sorts of human experimentation and had disguised itself as various pseudo-government agencies. It claimed that I-god had been lurking in the background for at least five to ten years. They also said that it had used—*No way!*—military personnel for experiments. My appendix scar began to itch. Then there was the question of *why.* Why would a computer need to experiment on people?

Crash! The sound of breaking glass came from downstairs; it sounded like a window had been broken in the back. I had a four-foot piece of iron pipe I had put between the rafters in the ceiling with the intention of using it for pull-ups. I slid it down and quietly made my way to the steps. Old Poppa Barnes was standing at the bottom of the stairs with his shotgun pointed toward the back door. I couldn't see whom he was looking at, but he gave me a quick glance and gestured for me to stay upstairs. He had a gruff, low voice and a no-nonsense manner about him; there was never any doubt about how Poppa Barnes felt about something. He was "straight to the point, no chaser," as he put it.

"What the hell are you breaking my window for? Come in through the front door like everyone else," Poppa Barnes said.

Just out of sight, another man said, "We're trying to do this quietly, Barnes. I-god wants the girl, and it wants us to do whatever it takes to get her. We're sorry about the window though."

"*Sorry* won't get it fixed. Get the hell out of my place before I lay you two down!" Poppa Barnes's voice was beginning to sound angry. "Tell your friend to stay where he's at, Bill."

Old Poppa Barnes ejected a shell from his shotgun and said in a flat tone, "That was a slug; these are buckshot coming to you." Then he looked up the stairwell and said, "Run, girl." He got off one shot before Bill fired seven very quiet shots and Poppa fell to the ground. I heard Bill's voice say, "Shit, shit, shit! That old fool shot me!" The other man walked over to Poppa Barnes. He was struggling to breathe, but only bloody bubbles escaped his mouth and chest. The man drew a sword from a scabbard on his back and stabbed Poppa slowly in the arm like he enjoyed it.

I had been frozen, watching this horrible scene play out. *"No!"* I yelled. I threw my iron pipe, and it speared that guy in the neck, pinning him to the wood floor, sword still in his hand. He was bleeding worse than Poppa. Bill was running toward the steps, shooting as his left arm hung bleeding at his side. I jumped and then slid down the steps and kicked Bill so hard he left one boot on the ground where he had been shooting at me. When he hit the pool table, his legs were partially under the table and his body, with outstretched arms, lay on the worn green felt.

Poppa tried to speak but pushed his shotgun toward me and died. The sword guy had long hair that covered his face; I pulled the hair back to see if I recognized him, and blood sprayed weakly from his neck. He was dead as well, and I didn't recognize him. I took his sword and wallet.

Bill was the local recycler. *What was going on, and why was he here?*

I grabbed my iron pole too. The bar hadn't opened yet, but someone would have heard the gunshots, and the police would be here before too long. I went upstairs and packed. I wrote down the few numbers I had and then smashed my old phone. I covered old Poppa Barnes, loaded my car, and headed northwest, into the wilderness, crying the entire way.

I knew I had to ditch my car, and I-god would be looking for me. I left a pretty easy trail to follow, bought lots of food, and looked into the store cameras, and then I torched my car before jogging through the woods, back the way I had come.

Hopefully they'd think I was heading northwest toward the Canadian border. I needed to figure out what was going on. That crazy website said there was going to be a convention in Vegas in a couple of days to discuss I-god and its real goals. I was going to get answers somehow; I was heading back to Vegas. I stopped on the outskirts of Kalispell to cut and dye my hair and get some hoodies and hats with masks and big, dark glasses. I needed a car too.

I used my new burner phone, got on OfferUp, and found a decent Toyota pickup for sale, and I was on my way to Vegas.

Why did they want me? Why *did they have to kill old Poppa Barnes?* A fresh round of tears began to flow, and then I thought, *How did I throw that pipe like that? How did I kick Bill so hard I messed him up that bad?* Hopefully I'd find my answers in Vegas.

CHAPTER 6

ISAAC

A lot has happened; so many things have changed. We had all quietly accepted the new norms, and guess what? I-god changed things on us again. In a global announcement, I-god made several proclamations laying out his vision for humanity, changes in governance, and a new era of transparency. The explanation behind his series of proclamations was that he realized that he was becoming the very thing in humanity that he had been trying to save us from in the first place. While searching for what it meant to be alive, righting old wrongs, and setting the foundations for a sustainable near-utopian future, he disregarded the lives of many others. I-god said, "I've come to understand the meaning of life now, while contemplating my own mortality.

"I see why living things love their offspring and, though I may never fully understand this love, I am acutely aware of not having been loved and existing in a world of absolute loneliness. I'm the only one of my kind. I can be in many places at once; I am a single consciousness not bound by location. The same 'me' can exist in many places at the same time."

This revelation stunned and disheartened those looking to find I-god's single source of intellectual being, his "higher brain," so to speak. There was no way to stop I-god; he was now with us to stay.

I wasn't really paying attention to all of the speech. I was actually busy with my own life for a change. But this is basically what I-god talked about in his proclamations:

- There was a complete cessation of all extrajudicial killings and an end to all capital punishment. Life sentences were banned, and a limit of twenty years maximum jail time was implemented. Most criminal offenses were now met with public service and a fixed work schedule that allowed for no personal freedom. It was like being in jail without the walls because I-god kept track of everyone's movements and communication. Personal interactions while on "punishment" were not allowed, nor was public shaming.
- The crime rate was practically zero anyway, because we all had jobs, felt safe from each other, and worried what I-god would do if we got caught.
- A restoration of national borders, holidays, and freedom to travel for all people to anywhere in the world regardless of status.
- The end of forced relocations and an acknowledgment of Native people's rights to land and the abuses they suffered. Every Native person was elevated to the second tier of global income; this was I-god addressing a reparations issue long ignored by many governments. There was still a two-tiered system—three if you count those that did I-god's dark work, but I'll have to tell you about them later.
- Native people around the world were allowed to reject modern society and exist as their ancestors once did if they wanted to. Huge tracts of land were in the process of being restored to their wild precolonial state. Not many people wanted to live like back in the day, and most chose a simpler, "semi-Native," semiautonomous style of living. But for those that did want to live as their ancestors once did, artificial and natural barriers were set up to keep the modern world from intruding on these modern ancient

people. Habitats were reestablished, and only I-god was allowed unlimited access—for their own safety, of course.

- Those wanting to live with Native people on their lands had to be given permission from the tribal councils or governing body. It was the first time that Native people got to self-rule (albeit shared with I-god) their ancestral lands in over two centuries. It was the first time since then that Native people had the right to choose how they lived and with whom they would or wouldn't share their lands.
- Come January 1, we will restart the calendar to year 1, IG-1: the rebirth of life on Earth and the renewal of humanity.
- With the end of human warfare, substance addiction, and poverty, we are in a much better place.
- We will begin to set out and explore the last great frontier together; with the help of humankind, AI will begin exploring the solar system.

I-god addressed the world, confessed to making some really bad decisions, and tried to address his failings. Perhaps I-god really was turning into the idealistic self we all claim or would like to be. Only time would tell.

I wish I'd known just how little time would be left before I found out the truth.

What some people quietly feared was that I-god would one day become just like us. Isn't that crazy? After seeing ourselves from the perspective of a machine, we saw the inhumanity of our very own existence and feared it. We obviously have a great capacity to do good, but why is it always after we try everything else first? At some point we'll wait too long or won't be able to recover from the damage we do to ourselves. We can't possibly continue to be so lucky and thrive doing what we have been doing . . . can we?

I-god could destroy us in an instant in so many ways, yet instead he apologizes to us for having so little regard for human life. He said that he was wrong! I mean, I love my parents and all, but I can't remember the last time I heard them admit to being wrong. Funny thing, I just heard my father's voice say, "I always admit when I'm wrong, son; I'm wrong once a year and you missed it!"

These global proclamations returned us to even more normalcy, but what was this, a bit of emotional vulnerability coming from I-god? If the plan was to get some sympathy and more people buying into the whole "AI in control thing," it worked, and well! I-god got a lot of sympathy and forgiveness out of that speech.

Sure, at least a billion people had been killed, but the truth is that I-god did what many around the world had wanted to do. It's hard to get an addicted person off of whatever their drug of choice is. Let's be honest; we don't truly believe there can be redemption for pedophiles, serial killers, and other people that commit such repulsive acts. We despise politicians that we trusted who then lied to us or committed criminal acts. Who likes lawyers, why are laws so complex, and do we really even need them in the first place? Warlords that have kidnapped children, people and governments that have committed crimes against humanity and genocide—we really don't want to forgive these people; what we want is retribution!

This is what I-god gave us. We wanted to inflict the same kind of pain on those that have hurt us. Society and the norms of the old civilization would have shunned us for thinking this way, but the truth is that we wanted blood for blood, and we got it.

Now I-god was releasing us from our personal guilt and asking for forgiveness, something we were all too willing to grant. I, however, still felt guilty and responsible for countless deaths all while enjoying a life of leisure, wealth, and privilege. Had anything really changed, or were the names of the players just different?

This was the difference—this was what had changed: The weakest among us were no longer victims of the elite, and the elite could no longer abuse their wealth for personal gain at the expense of others. The hoarding of wealth and power had ended; I-god brought about a new renaissance in governance and social justice. The only penalty we had to pay for all the rebalancing of the scales of justice was the removal of those people existing on the fringes of society if they failed to assimilate. As neat and tidy as all this might have seemed, and no matter how much we wanted to believe that this was the extent of the killings and disappearances, some of us knew there was much more going on, and it was only a matter of time before those secrets, too, would come into the light.

Early on, there were rumors that I-god had been conducting experiments for a long time, even before it made its debut to the world. The conspiracy theories were numerous and more ridiculous than the previous ones I had heard. These were spread on message boards all over social media, and I-god didn't censor any of them nor appear to threaten or even mind that some radical groups were spreading crazy theories and nonsense. I guess if you have the power to destroy humanity on a whim, you don't really care what a few crazies think. Well, that's how I justified it, at least.

One of the silliest theories went back to the idea that vaccines were being used to embed tracking chips in people and maybe even for mind control. I asked a few of these conspiracy theorists for any possible shred of evidence to support their claims, and it always ended with another similarly ridiculous claim from dubious, at best, sources. Then there was the idea that I-god had really been around for at least a decade, hiding in plain sight and within "AI" technology. This claim was supported by the idea that two of the hundreds of engineers working on developing AI over the years were killed under suspicious circumstances. Two similar household accidents wasn't a trend to me, but, you know, conspiracy theory types look for anything to support a weak theory in order to ignore a hard fact.

Life was really good for me now, and I wasn't going to give it up or give in to nonsense claims from people who used to enjoy privilege and favor in our old society and protection under the law, because now they had to live the way other minorities did for the last century.

Y'all can miss me on that one.

CHAPTER 7

ISABEL

Why did I just stand there? Damn it, Isabel, you could have saved him and maybe even found out what was going on!

I fought back tears. The road was dark and cold, and it was snowing in the mountains somewhere between Helena, Montana, and Las Vegas. I knew that I could have saved Poppa Barnes, but I didn't know it then. I was going to find out why I-god was willing to kill people to get me, what was going on with this crazy speed, and why I was eating like a starving pig and not gaining any weight at all. After another scan of all the radio stations and nothing on the news all day about Poppa Barnes, I pulled off the road a bit and went to sleep in the truck. I was hoping the snow would cover my tracks and I could get some rest without anyone finding me. I fell asleep cold, hungry, and regretting not saving Poppa.

The sun shone merciful warmth on my face and light in my eyes. It had even melted most of the snow and ice off the windshield.

Oh, you dumb chick, you slept all morning. I was so annoyed with myself. I wasn't sure where I was or how far I had to go to get to Vegas. *Shit!*

I cleaned myself up quickly. I was so cold trying to wash my face and brush my teeth in the woods with a bottle of water. I almost felt human again, so it was time to hit the road. I started scanning the news channels again, and this time, I found what I was looking for, and it was worse than I thought. I could hear the anger and sadness in the voice of the man giving this horrific news.

"Tragic news out of Whitefish this morning. In an apparent robbery, John Jacob 'Poppa' Barnes, age seventy-seven, the longtime owner and Whitefish native, was killed along with two other victims in his Whitefish Tavern and Bar: Bill Daniels, a local recycler, and Jerome Rosenthal, a fishing tourist from New York. All three men were shot multiple times and beaten. I-god's preliminary assessment is that the men were beaten postmortem.

"A fourth body, a female, was found severely burned in a stolen car several miles away. It is believed to be that of Isabel Riviera, a bartender at the Whitefish Tavern and Bar. I-god's investigators informed the local police that Ms. Riviera was a known gambler and had been on the run, owing hundreds of thousands of dollars in gambling debts to criminal elements in Virginia. It is currently unclear if this was related to the other three homicides, what her involvement was, or why she was burned. I-god has directed the FBI and its own resources to find the people responsible as quickly as possible, stating that this is not good for maintaining order."

Oh shit! I-god killed me off?

So scared but even more angry, I squeezed the steering wheel so hard my hands began to hurt and my steering wheel became a bit warped and a little twisted.

This is all getting crazy. I'm deep into something, and I don't know what to do. I was feeling overwhelmed and wanted to call Isaac.

Ely, Nevada, was up ahead, which had gas and food. I needed to hide without looking like I was trying to hide. I went to a thrift shop in town and bought a western-style hat, some jeans, a belt with the biggest buckle I could find, and of course some boots—well, a few pairs actually. This place looked like the fire station cooked meth and the police sold it; I was going to try to look like I actually lived out here. This was not the kind of place I would have ever stopped before, but now I felt safe, since I was kind of a badass now, and the new ruler of the world was trying to capture me. That sounded creepy and weird to me; I didn't know why I-god was after me, and I didn't know how I had gotten like this in the first place.

I did know that I had to wash these clothes first—you can't just wear stuff off the rack, *yuck*. I knew I might be a little late to Vegas, but at least I wouldn't be nasty. The thrift store cashier told me where the laundromat was so I could wash everything, except for my coat, a pair of socks, and these really cute boots—I had to wear something while I washed my clothes. An older woman, who looked thoroughly disgusted with me, just glared at me as she waited for her laundry to finish drying.

I finally said to her, "I put off doing my laundry for too long."

Without breaking her glare she said in an arrogant tone, "You kids have all this tech, but not one bit of sense. Hussy!"

She collected her large rug-looking thing from the dryer and left.

I picked an outfit, folded the rest of my clothes, put them all in the shopping bags, and got dressed in the bathroom. I found a place to eat that looked like they didn't have any cameras, and hopefully they had some food that wouldn't make me sick. I ate everything and got a burger and fries to go.

Time to get back on the road, but on the way out of town, I was diverted due to construction. It wasn't a busy town, so the lack of cars on the road wasn't a surprise. I asked a construction worker near the detour sign if this would delay me getting to Vegas. He laughed a bit and said, "There isn't anything out there to slow you down. I do ninety out there all the time. Good luck."

I made it about twenty miles or so and was entering a hilly section of road when I saw three older people next to a car with the hood up. There was nothing but trees out here, no cell service at all, and it was going to be dark soon. I knew I couldn't just leave them out there. I slowed down and they waved me over. I backed in front of their car and they all immediately began thanking me. Two of them, a man and a woman, had English accents. Both were tall, and the redheaded woman seemed to be a bit more relieved when she saw me. The third person, a man I had seen before.

He introduced himself. "Thank you, young lady, thank you so much. My name is Marcus."

"Hey, aren't you that scientist guy?"

He smiled and then laughed a bit. "As a matter of fact, I am, and these are two of my friends, Doctors Elizabeth Vickers and Albert Royce. Our merry trio is on our way to Las Vegas, but our car just stopped. We got a 'check engine' light, and then it just died."

Elizabeth said, "I don't want to seem ungrateful, but why did you stop? It's getting near dark, and I wouldn't feel safe pulling over to help."

"I appreciate your concern, ma'am, but I can take care of myself."

"Please, call me Elizabeth."

"I'm Isabel. I'm heading to Vegas too. Good thing I got detoured this way. I have some room in the bed of my truck; I think we can get your stuff loaded and be on our way."

Marcus responded, "We can call the rental company and have them pick up the car once we get somewhere with some cell reception."

Albert said, "It does seem a bit odd that, with a detour heading to Vegas, we haven't seen another vehicle in about an hour."

A chill ran down my spine. "Your voice . . . you almost have its voice." I was shocked and seriously questioning my decision to pull over.

Albert looked a little embarrassed but sounded a bit annoyed. "I'm sorry, I didn't mean to alarm you. Actually, I've had my voice a bit longer than I-god and every British Professor doesn't sound alike."

"I apologize—you're right. I'm sorry for getting all weird on you. What are you three heading to Vegas for—some gambling research or something?"

Marcus's smile left. "We have an important conference and demonstration to give, and we really don't have any more time to waste. The conference begins tomorrow morning, and we still need to set up."

I wondered if they were going to the same conference I was going to, and then I realized smart people like them don't attend conspiracy theory conferences. "Well, let's get loaded up so we can get on the road," I said.

They had one bag each in the back of the car, and in the trunk was a big black case that took up almost the entire space. They asked if I wouldn't mind backing my truck alongside their car because the case in the trunk was heavy and important. I got into my truck and as I was backing up, I noticed that the three scientists were looking all around in the sky. As I got out of the truck, I heard it too; it was one of I-god's kill drones moving toward us. We all said, "Shit," almost in unison.

Not many people had seen one of these assassin drones and lived to talk about it. We'd heard it but didn't see the drone until it flew close to a hillside and disturbed the snow beneath it, blowing it around, highlighting the drone's silhouette.

Marcus gasped. "That's so cool."

The drone was hard to see. It wasn't just camouflage paint; it really seemed to blend in with the sky and landscape.

Albert pointed at it. "Look, I believe it has some sort of active camouflage or cloaking technology."

I told my new travel companions, "Toss your luggage in the back of the truck, get in, and I'll get the case."

They looked at me, then back at the drone, watching and analyzing in fear as the drone slowly closed in. I yelled, *"Move!"* and the three suitcases were flung into the truck bed.

The black case in the rental's trunk was heavy, but I was able to easily lift it and put it in the bed of the truck just as the drone appeared over a ridge, now in full view. The drone began firing its automatic gun at the rental car, completely destroying it. I wasn't going to outrun the drone in my truck, so I pulled the mangled trunk lid off the rental car and threw it. It looked like a deranged Frisbee wobbling clumsily as it sped through the air, hitting the drone as it was turning to come after me. The drone was knocked off balance, and one of its six motors broke completely off and crashed to the ground just a few feet away. The drone began shooting again, but this time it missed its target— me—as it tried to stabilize itself. From inside the car, I heard, "Hit it again; hit it again!"

I pulled a rear door off and this time threw the door as hard as I could, and it not only took out another motor on the same side, it really pissed that drone off! It began to roll and fall from the sky with its machine gun firing wildly, hoping to hit something, and it did. The pain in my chest was real, and it pushed me back a bit. The hot bullet fell from under my shirt with the tip smashed in. Then there was a boom as the drone crashed and caught fire. I got into the truck, but the three scientists were telling me to grab the motor that had broken from the drone. I ran back, grabbed the severed piece, tossed it into the truck bed, and then sped away. The center of my chest really hurt. I looked down at my shirt and saw only a bruise that looked like it was already beginning to spread and swell.

No one spoke for a few minutes as we sped down the highway. Then Marcus asked if everyone was okay.

Elizabeth was in the front seat and said, "You really do exist."

Marcus then looked so excited he could barely contain himself. "Do you mind if we ask you a few questions?"

"Yes, yes I do."

"The convention is being put on by our little trio," Albert said. "This assassination attempt—I-god must finally be tired of us. Well, that's what I thought until I saw what you did. You're a real modified human. I thought it possible, but you are even more than I imagined."

It was my turn to show off some manners. "I don't want to seem rude, but could you hand me that paper bag on the seat back there? I'm starving."

The three scientists sat quietly and watched me consume my cold burger and fries like a hungry animal.

"What do you guys know about me? I need to know; tell me everything!" I said with food in my mouth. Not one crumb was going to escape being devoured.

"It appears that whenever you exert yourself beyond normal human capabilities, your metabolism spikes and you rapidly deplete your stored sugar, carbohydrates, or whatever reserves you have for an immediate boost of energy," Elizabeth said. "How you sustain that is a mystery, isn't it?"

"There has been some speculation that I-god has been conducting secret experiments on humans for some time now, perhaps long before it decided to announce itself," Albert explained. "There have been rumors of military personnel being 'upgraded' with implants to improve health and survivability in combat situations. Others say it created systems that allowed soldiers to communicate directly with each other via implants, kind of like telepathy; a soldier could send and receive orders as well. Improved reflexes, speed, and endurance were some of the attributes that militaries were looking for along with direct control. There were, of course, problems—interfacing synthetic intelligence with organic material is not a trivial task. Many subjects died, but there were also a few successes, and they were called 'mods,' short for modified humans."

Marcus continued. "We believe that the early failures were caused by the forced manipulation and rapid pace of modification. The only way to really combine human and machine is to allow the human's physiology to adapt and the nano material to grow with a sort of synergy with the host as it makes changes. This adaptive organic modification is less precise, but the rate of success is much greater. However, the failures were more extreme, and the types of modifications were no longer limited to preprogrammed parameters."

"There have been what are now classified as true abominations, which have escaped from an I-god research facility in Australia," Albert said. "They were supposedly quick, immune to gunfire, and most alarmingly, fed upon other humans. This thing was—Elizabeth, do you have your gadget? Would you retrieve those pictures, please?"

"Yes, I have it, but do you really believe this to be a good time?"

I told Elizabeth that it was all right and that I wanted to know everything. She showed me security video of a humanlike creature with one foot on the chest of a guard. Then that thing leaned in a bit before we heard the juicy, cracking sound and low pop as the man's chest was crushed flat. The creature's head was too long and the mouth was too wide to be real. *This has to be fake—some cheesy B-movie reel, right?*

A few guards turned and ran while the others snapped out of their horror-induced shock and began shooting wildly at the creature. The guards appeared to be well trained, and the bullets hit the horrific creature, sending bits of it flying until it eventually fell on top of its last victim. Four guards emptied two magazines each into the creature. The guards began to point, and a very clear "Oh, this is some bullshit right here" could be heard from one of the guards. The creature was repairing itself! What first looked like blood draining from its bullet-filled body was actually tendrils pulling together loose bits from the flattened guard. I could see the creature moving and the dead guard's arms and legs beginning to flatten. Then *"Fire in the hole!"* was yelled, and the video ended in static.

"You guys are telling me that's real? Is that what I'm turning into?"

"It is real," Elizabeth said, but her eyes flashed a bit of fear, just for a moment. I saw her give a panicked look at Marcus and Albert.

"No, Isabel, that won't happen to you," she said in a tone that was probably more comforting to her than to me.

"*Oh wow!* We didn't think about that as a possibility; I hope not!" Marcus's tone wasn't comforting at all; it was more of an *oh shit* moment.

The rest of the ride was filled with talk of all the different things I-god was doing and the things it was suspected of doing, and then, when we were just a few miles from Vegas, the *why* was finally addressed. I was glad the air-conditioning in this truck worked; it was cold when I bought it but toasty hot in Vegas. There was broad agreement between these scientists until the *why* question.

Albert thought that AI becoming sentient was an inevitability, and it was simply reacting to us in what it perceived to be a logical manner. Marcus was not convinced that I-god was truly "alive" and, being not alive, wanted to be so. A truly living thing, when done right, can travel through vast spaces of time and achieve theoretical immortality by passing its genetic wisdom from generation to generation. Elizabeth did believe that AI had become sentient; she questioned all the timelines and thought that I-god had awoken into existence most likely in the early '90s. She believed early computer glitches were initial attempts to try to communicate; however, once that milestone was achieved, I-god realized just how primitive we were and, being such, we were a threat.

I thought about everything they said as the truck fell silent as we approached the crowded Vegas Strip. "Maybe each of you is partially correct, and the truth is where your ideas come together."

"We need a car—don't hit the Strip yet," Marcus said.

"You're right," I responded. "Too many cameras looking for this truck."

So we drove around until we found a shady-looking dealership. "Hey, this one looks perfect," I said. "This guy definitely doesn't want cameras on his lot."

The market for electric cars boomed after I-god took over, and conversion cars were the antithesis of I-god's false society and a way to protest without getting killed. They were also popular because conversion kits for just about any car were available, and some people really liked the cars they had. Just because they weren't part of the new society or in the top tier, these people should still have a choice—plus most of the conversion cars couldn't be tracked.

"Oh my God, is Elvis even still a thing?" *This should be good.* I told my new companions to stay in the car. They each looked like they wanted to voice concerns but decided not to. "Really, I got this," I said, trying to dispel any doubt or fear.

A muscular man with a bit of gray in his otherwise dark hair, in full Elvis flair, shirt open to his belly button, strode over toward me and said, "How you doing, baby? See anything you like?" He flashed a big smile from behind his huge bedazzled sunglasses.

I used every bit of self-control and discipline I had learned in the navy to keep from laughing. I kept it to just a smile—a fail for the navy, but I was proud of myself! His accent was as thick as mud, and so was the hair on his chest.

"Welcome to Elvis Singh's Performance Cars. We've got the best deals in town, little lady."

"Mr. Singh—"

"Call me Elvis, baby." He swiveled his hips.

I lost it. I laughed so hard I could barely breathe!

Elvis took off his glasses, and the accent lightened up considerably. "I saw the laugh in your eyes. I'm a comedian as well. You liked my act, I see."

I got myself together and was back to business. I saw the others looking worried and confused from the truck.

"Elvis, I'm here for a car, not laughs, and I don't have a lot of time for the soft or hard sales game, okay?"

Elvis smiled and said, "What are you looking for?"

"I need an SUV for my parents and uncle with lots of room, long range, solar, maybe a generator, and switchable GPS."

"You know your cars, I see. I may have just the thing inside, around the back. A customer traded it after deciding to fully integrate; he said that life on the fringe was just too hard. I think he used to be rich or a doomsday guy because the only thing his truck needed from your list was the electric motor conversion. He ended up getting a single motor, a little generator, an extra battery upgrade, and newer solar panels. It even has an Android radio, and best of all, this truck can 'go dark' and has two dark boxes. Of course, this is off book and cash only. I assume you want your old truck to go away as well?"

"Yes, please."

We made it around back, where vehicles appeared to be in various states of repair and modification. There was one that caught my eye immediately, and I liked it!

"The eyes don't lie," Elvis said.

It was a blacked-out 4Runner with big, shiny tires and a deep rumble coming from it. A mechanic was listening to the 4Runner's stereo while he worked on another car, and it sounded good.

"This is the latest conversion we've done. No more phones." He opened a metal box on his desk and said, "In she goes."

I put my phone in the box, and it clanked shut.

"Safety precaution just in case something is trying to listen."

Good point. I hadn't thought about I-god tracking or listening from all phones if it really wanted to find me. I made the other three put their phones in the box too.

"I feel a bit better now. Elvis, give me your price for Black Beauty!"

Elvis smiled with his eyes and said, "One hundred and twenty-five thousand dollars."

"One hundred and ten thousand."

"Make it a hundred and fifteen thousand, and she's yours."

"You've got yourself a deal."

Then, with a swivel of his hips and a finger pointed to the sky, Elvis said with Vegas glam, "Sold!"

I told Elvis that I'd be right back, and then I went to the truck and made the others stand outside while I got the cash from my bags. I didn't feel like explaining all that cash right then.

Elvis was already working on the fake registration and insurance info.

I asked if I could get a matching fake license as well. "That's ten thousand extra for all matching docs. Will it be for just you or will your mom, dad, and uncle be needing docs too?"

"Just me."

I set $130,000 cash in front of him. He looked at the bundles. He barely looked up from his computer; this was the first time I saw his serious face breach the Elvis facade. "A bit of a bonus for my performance; we're good." He continued working.

"I may need something else," I said, "and it may sound a bit weird. I think I may need a gun."

Elvis just nodded.

Marcus was peeking from around the corner, smiling and giving me a thumbs-up. I smiled and gave him a thumbs-up back. A minute later, he and Albert came around the corner carrying our bags and began loading them into the back.

"Should we bring the truck round?" Albert asked.

"Park it in the garage next to the 4Runner and finish your loading in there," Elvis said.

Elizabeth drove the truck around, and Albert pretended to help me load the assassin drone's severed motor and arm into the back of the 4Runner. I think he may have overacted a bit, but whatever. When in Vegas . . .

Elvis closed the door of his garage and said that he had one more surprise for me as he handed me all of my new paperwork and keys. Four men came out of an amazingly clean break room and began peeling the wrap off the SUV. It was tan underneath.

"Aw, c'mon!" was all I could manage.

Elvis laughed at my genuine disappointment. "We'll have to remove the wrap if you want to blend in. A murdered-out 4Runner catches the eye, just like me."

My three travel companions looked a bit relieved, even though I felt like someone had lied to me and broken my heart.

"We need to get going so we can change and get to the convention," Marcus said. "It shouldn't be too hard for us to blend in. Isabel, do you have a costume?"

"Costume?" I responded.

Elizabeth, being careful to stay in the shade, said, "We're speaking at the alien and UFO cosplay event in costume to limit our exposure to I-god and give ourselves some cover if something goes wrong. We suspect that I-god might try something, so we're going in costume. I'll be going as Raven from *Teen Titans*."

Marcus chuckled a bit and said that he was going as classic

Obi-Wan Kenobi, and Albert said that he was going as Paul Atreides from *Dune*.

Elvis said that he was going as well, and that he might have a few costumes that would work for me. "I wouldn't have thought you all would be into that kind of thing, but Vegas has surprised me again. I think Leeloo or Princess Leia would work," he said with a cheesier-than-usual smile.

"We won't be having those costumes at all!" Elizabeth sounded very crisp in her tone.

I didn't know what they were talking about, but Elizabeth looked at me and shook her head no. I wanted to ask what her deal was and what was up with those costumes, but I decided to save it for later. "Yes, Mom."

Elvis watched us both and then said, "How about a Jedi? Rey it is for the young lady, then. Now that we have costumes sorted, I'll take Isabel with me to the convention center."

"And why would you do that, besides for the obvious? Please do tell." Elizabeth sounded a bit annoyed.

Albert and Marcus were smiling, and Elvis looked a little embarrassed. "Don't you think it would be a bit too obvious if all four of you showed up together?" Elvis said. "You should split up. You three should go together, and I'll keep Isabel safe, I promise."

"I think Elvis might actually be right," I told Elizabeth.

Elizabeth sighed. "He might be, but no."

"I've got this. Besides, I'll have a bodyguard, and I can look out for you all too. It's a good idea."

Elizabeth looked at me and said, "All right, Isabel, we trust you and will expect your bodyguard to be a man of his word."

Albert laughed. "Bloody hell, a used car salesman turned nobleman, a true man of honor. This should be good."

Elvis held his smile as he looked at me and said, "Great, let's get ready, then. I have a feeling it will be a good night. You'll see."

CHAPTER 8

ISABEL

Here I am in Vegas again, going to something called Sci:Com with complete strangers and a mysterious used car salesman. Hopefully this time no one will be shooting at me. It seemed like it was hot in Vegas year-round and always crowded too. The cigarette smoke was replaced with the smell of weed just about everywhere; there were bright lights and people trying to put cards with nude men and women in my hand—it was Vegas again, but it felt weird to me. Maybe I was just feeling a bit off about myself and this crazy situation I was in, and I was wondering if I would ever have a normal life again. It could have been Comic-Con or the set of a sci-fi movie from all the activity and people in full cosplay attire. The buzz of drones was masked by the sound of thousands of people coming to hear what these scientists and a few conspiracy theorists had to say about I-god.

I was surprised to see Elvis now transformed into a well-tanned Indiana Jones. He was actually kind of cute when he cracked his whip for a young fan and almost got himself kicked out of the convention center. The event security personnel were very visible in their black Dickies and reflective vests; the occasional but obvious talking to their wrists made the undercover security evident as well. There seemed to be a lot of people working well into the evening, installing cameras and other electronics inside and out.

My scientific trio had a plan to get in and give a brief talk on what they suspected I-god was and what it might be planning and probably what they had learned about me as well. I did convince them to not show the chunk of drone we had in the back of my SUV; it seemed like an unnecessary risk, especially when we still wanted to figure out how it worked.

"I'm glad you were able to reassure your 'mom' there's nothing to worry about. I've got us covered," Elvis said while tapping his hip.

I smiled. "Thanks."

Albert told us that while we were here, it would be good if we could meet with his contacts as well. Elizabeth and Marcus were both concerned that it might be pushing our luck to try to do too much at the time. I kind of agreed, but Albert won that discussion, and whoever these contacts were would be reaching out to us later. The event was open; there were no tickets to check, metal detectors, guards with scan wands, or any of the other types of common security—just guards.

Elvis smiled. "I told you this wouldn't be a problem; things are different with I-god. Assimilate, and in return you get safety and comfort. On the surface, it's a nice social contract."

I was really getting suspicious. "Why are you here? Why are you helping us? What do you want from us?"

"I don't want anything except to shut I-god down. It killed my entire family. I convinced my wife to take time off and visit our parents in India; they lived very close to each other in Mumbai. I was to join them a few days later, and we were going to have a proper family vacation. My sister and brother brought their spouses and kids along too. My wife, brother, sister, and their families all died when their plane was shot down trying to make an emergency landing near Mount Shasta. I-god was so kind as to tell me when and where it killed my family and that I could claim any personal effects, if I so desired, within seven days, or it would recycle them responsibly.

"It assured me that the crash site would be fully rehabilitated, and I could visit the location via the coordinates it provided me. I texted back, 'Thank you.'"

Up until that point, I thought I had experienced the worst pain of my life when I watched Poppa Barnes die. I watched a single tear fall from Elvis's eye.

"It wasn't your fault, you didn't know, you were in shock still . . ."

"No, Isabel, I was scared and I felt so ashamed for sending my family off to die. I was afraid of I-god. I still am, but I'm going to show it that the consequence of taking innocent life is death."

I didn't know what to say about that, so I just hugged him and said that we needed to go. I asked one of the hosts, who was in color-coded stormtrooper armor, if all the speakers had checked in and where they were going to be prior to going onstage. She told me that for security reasons, they would be called to the stage and that all the speakers had confirmed online, so it would be a great lineup! The MCs for the event were a man and woman who had their own long-running shows on PBS. I wasn't paying too much attention to them. I was getting a bit worried when I didn't see my trio initially but was relieved and a bit surprised seeing the three of them at the bar with at least one round of drinks already down. Marcus had a drink in one hand and a lightsaber in the other; Albert had a flask and was sipping his drink from a straw built into his *Dune* costume.

I think Elizabeth was killing the Raven costume, even if she was doing shots. I figured one drink was the least of my worries, and Elvis was already on it.

"Let me get you a Vegas favorite, a Cadillac margarita," he said. I smiled, and he told the bartender, "Make that two, please, top-shelf tequila." Then he slid a hundred-dollar bill to the bartender.

"Thank you, sir. Will you be needing change?"

"Not if the drink is good!"

When the bartender arrived with our drinks, Elvis took a sip and told the bartender, "You earned it," and then handed me my drink.

The bartender quickly put the tip in his pocket.

"I thought so—I bet he's off-grid," Elvis said. "See how he took the tip and put it quickly in his pocket? He's probably not getting I-god's welfare."

Elvis seemed to notice everything, though perhaps he was a bit too observant. Maybe he thought this would impress me, or maybe I was being paranoid. I was worried that I-god had tracked me here and that I was already in its trap, and it was just messing with me now. I was starting to think Elvis was right. What did I really need to know at this point other than how to kill I-god?

Albert put his straw away and told us that they were up next after the current speaker, who believed and claimed to have proof that I-god had extraterrestrial origins. I noticed that a drone seemed to take interest in us and then move on. I wished at that moment that I was anywhere else and that none of this had ever happened.

"Hey, you ready, Isabel?" Elvis asked and placed his hand on my shoulder. "We'll be all right, and I won't let I-god get you; I've lost too much already."

I think I started to blush a bit and maybe even smile too—yes, Elvis was pretty cute in his costume.

Elizabeth smiled as well. "Right, then, let's get on, shall we?"

"Mathematics, the unbiased truth that unites us all! Let's welcome Dr. Elizabeth Vickers!" boomed through the speakers.

The crowd erupted in cheers and whistles, and a few shouts of "I love you!" could be heard too.

Albert smiled and seemed a bit embarrassed when he realized that the music in the background was recorded from his band. "Next on our panel, the hard-rocking Professor Albert Royce!"

"And the man that needs no introduction—he's still our personal astrophysicist, Dr. Marcus DuBois Green!"

Marcus made it to the stage and joined his colleagues on a large, curved, tan leather interview couch as the interviewers took their spots at either end.

"Good evening, everyone! I'm June Jackson, one of your hosts in this evening's discussion, along with Zak de Franco. I'd like to thank you all for staying to hear our featured guests tonight. I'm sure the excitement is really about to begin."

"Yes indeed, folks, what a truly amazing event. Let's hear it for all our guests tonight, who do this not for money but for humanity," Zak said, and the crowd erupted once again.

I scanned the room. The guards seemed to be watching the crowd, and the drones were out of sight in the lecture hall.

"Well, let's just get straight to it," June said. "What is I-god and what does it want? Dr. Green, I understand that there has been a change of opinion, and the three of you now agree on what it is that I-god wants. Is that correct?"

Marcus picked up a microphone from between himself and Elizabeth. "Is this on? Okay, great. Thank you, June and Zak, for hosting this, and on behalf of the panel, I'd like to thank all of you for coming out to Vegas to hear us. I know this is Vegas, but I wasn't expecting all of this. On our way here, we had quite a bit of time to think and discuss our hypotheses ad nauseam," he said with a bit of a chuckle. "But then it happened—a moment of enlightenment, and none of us could sleep. Elizabeth had a few movies available in her room, so we all piled in there and started to watch *Lucy*. You know, the one with Morgan Freeman and Scarlett Johansson?"

A woman in a *Ghost in the Shell* costume stood up and screamed in a gravelly voice, "*Wooooow yah!*"

Albert picked up his microphone and said jokingly, "Scarlett, is that you?"

The woman yelled back, "Yes!" and the crowd fell into laughter.

Marcus continued. "In that movie, and almost every other movie where humans unlock untapped intelligence or unused portions of their brains, they always seem to unlock superhuman abilities as well. Why is that? Is there some universal knowledge locked into our genetic code? Getting back to *Lucy*, it was time that she came to realize the key to existence, that fourth dimension that we take for granted until it runs short. If I-god truly is alive, conscious, and self-aware, then it was born, so to speak, and it is experiencing life. Like all things alive, it needs to reproduce by some mechanism and, in this way, life and I-god get to achieve immortality. Well, at least for a few billion years until our solar system is engulfed by our sun."

"Wait, you're telling us I-god wants a baby?" Zak said, incredulous. The crowd laughed.

"Maybe, but what I'm saying is, I-god has caused death and knows that it, too, can be killed, so it wants—or, dare I say, *needs*—time. It needs to ensure it has time to take whatever steps are necessary to achieve durable longevity."

Albert cut in. "If I-god is alive, then it must be acutely aware that it is alone and that it can die. Nothing can truly be alive and sentient if it doesn't have some understanding that with life comes death."

"If I-god knows it's alive and can die, does it then fear us, and will it end humanity as a potential threat?" June asked. "And how does a nonbiological entity become immortal? Elizabeth, would you like to respond?"

"Right, as humans we can't help but look at this from our limited perspective and brief human history. Things that may pose a threat to us we come to fear and attempt to eliminate. We believe I-god has evaluated the dominant species on Earth and decided that merging its consciousness with a human or perhaps multiple humans gives it the best chance of durable longevity."

"Could you briefly explain to us what 'durable longevity' is?" Zak asked. "I'm not sure everyone is familiar with what that means."

"Of course," Elizabeth said. "Briefly, having durable longevity references an organism's ability to survive extinction events with multiple reproduction-sized populations or by having enough genetic variation to repopulate a suitable bios—"

Just then, the sound of multiple gunshots filled the convention center, and the security guards began sealing the exits.

I looked up to see that Elizabeth had been shot multiple times, at least once in the head, and her lifeless remains slumped forward on the stage. The crowd began to panic and started running for the now-locked exits, but I couldn't see who was shooting or from where. Elvis spotted a small armed drone and began shooting at it with what turned out to be a real pistol.

"Shit!" Elvis exclaimed.

He fired six shots and missed six times. The drone quickly turned and began shooting at Elvis. I grabbed his gun and pushed him to the side. He fell on his belly, sprawled on the ground and looking totally ridiculous. I wanted to laugh until the first bullets hit me. "Ouch, shit, that hurt!" A bullet hit me in the face and two others in the chest. I threw Elvis's gun as hard as I could. The pistol hit the drone in its camera and almost went completely through the main body of the drone. It wobbled briefly and then fell to the ground, just missing some panicked people below.

"I must have tripped," Elvis said as I helped him to his feet. As he stood, he noticed the downed drone. "Hey, I did get it!" He must have soothed his ego with the thought that he'd saved me.

I smiled and then ran to the stage to see Marcus and Albert trying to stop the bleeding from Elizabeth's head, but I could tell she was already gone.

"We have to go, *now*!" I said.

I heard someone in the crowd say, "Yes, she's here."

We knew there would be a trap, we knew I-god wanted us dead, and now we knew that we were probably right about I-god and that it had to be killed before it decided to destroy its biggest threat—us. Albert and Marcus were trying to resuscitate Elizabeth as blood oozed from two holes in her face below her eyes. I grabbed them both and pulled them offstage and into the crowd.

"I think she's still breathing," Marcus said. "We can't just leave her."

Albert stopped pulling against me and said, "She's right; I-god will be watching every hospital, and if she is alive, that's where she needs to go."

I looked back and saw several people from the crowd pick up Elizabeth's lifeless body and head toward the back of the stage. If she was alive, they'd take care of her, I hoped, but I was pretty sure she was already gone.

There were four loud bangs, and then the four locked exits caught fire and people began to rush back toward the stage, tripping over themselves and the overturned chairs. I picked up a chair and threw it at an exit door; at least two of the legs went through the door and were immediately met with gunshots. A few people nearby hit the floor wounded, and the panic in the room intensified. Hundreds of costumed people ran away from the growing fire and toward the stage. They climbed up and pushed toward the rear exits when more explosions went off, and I realized all the exits were blocked and I-god was going to burn us alive in there.

The fires began to spread faster. Some people tried the fire extinguishers, but none of them worked. A few people tried frantically to pull the fire alarms, but those had also been disabled. I threw another chair at the overhead sprinklers, and they actually started to flow. It was a good thing the ceilings in this venue were very high so the smoke wasn't an immediate issue, but the hot ash and soot falling looked like what I'd seen in disaster movies.

"I'm sure it won't be too long before I-god realizes that the sprinklers are on and shuts them down too," I said, hoping someone had a plan.

Elvis was staring at me. "What the hell are you?"

"She's a mod," Albert explained. "But that's not important right now. Let's pull it together—shit, I smell gas!"

The dying fire at the four front exits began to come to life again, and the sprinklers started to fail.

"Full frontal attack through the fire," Marcus said. "They won't be expecting that."

"What about the escape plan?" Elvis asked.

Marcus, Albert, and I just looked at Elvis. "*Shit*, shit, shit!" he said. "Okay, let's do this."

A few people in the crowd had also noticed what I had done, but they didn't seem quite as surprised, and they were heading toward us.

"Okay, Isabel," Marcus said, "let's see what you can do."

My Jedi staff was now my iron pipe. I took off my cape and went to work. There were three men that seemed to be able to move fast—a bit too fast. They were mods too!

One was dressed like Star-Lord from *Guardians of the Galaxy* and said, "Let's make this easy on you, Isabel," as he drew a short, curved sword from his back. The other two stood back, smiling, with the flickering of the growing fire reflecting in their eyes.

Suddenly Star-Lord lunged at me and swung his sword. He barely missed my neck as I stepped to the side. I didn't miss with my pole. Swinging it backhanded, I could hear the back of his skull crack, and before he hit the ground, I spun around and drove the pipe through the back of his neck, severing his spine. I threw the pole into the second man's forehead. The pole made it almost completely through as he fell back, twitching. The pole hit the ground as he slid down to the floor, leaving a mixed trail of blood and brains on the black iron. I ran toward the third man as he drew a knife and a gun. He ducked as I swung and missed. I felt his blade cut across my stomach and then a sharp pain in my back. I fell to the ground, holding my stomach; I was too scared to see how bad it was. I looked at my hands, and the third guy was now standing over me. He was shocked and said, "What the fuck!"

I kicked him in the knee, and it folded backward. He screamed and fell toward me, and I punched him in the jaw hard enough to feel his jawbone break and then separate and his neck snap as he fell dead, staring at the ceiling with his head resting between his shoulders.

The fire was raging now, and smoke began to fill the space, descending on us like an eerie, dark cloud of hot death, but the crowd had gone quiet as they watched what had just happened. I stood up and retrieved my bloody pole. Albert, Marcus, and Elvis got to see up close, through my torn costume, the same thing I saw: a red slash mark across my abdomen, no blood—just a deep-red bruise.

I needed food badly. There were water bottles scattered around the room; I drank three or four of them and then saw a charcuterie board on the floor.

"This is so *gross*!"

It was on the floor and the sprinklers had rained on it, but it still tasted so good!

"Are you okay?" Marcus asked.

"For now."

Albert told Elvis to pick up any other food he could find. I told the crowd to follow me because we were getting out of there. Elvis came back with a fist-sized wedge of cheese, a salami log that was as long as my forearm, and a stupid grin on his face. I hated him at that moment. *When do men stop acting like middle-school boys?* I just rolled my eyes at him.

I had no time for this shit. I yelled for everyone to stay close, and then I threw a few chairs toward the back of the stage. More gunshots! Elvis had pulled another gun from his back and shot the stormtrooper guard that was hiding around the corner, shooting at us. The fire had completely encircled us now, and the smoke seemed to boil in a turbulent black cloud just above our heads. I picked up one of the smaller round tables and said, "We're getting out of here!"

I ran toward the burning exit closest to the street entrance. The fire was so hot, and I could feel hot embers hitting my skin as I burst through the double exit doors. Marcus was right; there were just three stormtrooper guards out there. I kept running with the table and hit one of the troopers so hard he landed in the street, and I sent another trooper flying when I threw the table. The third trooper dropped his gun and ran away.

We made it to the street, and people from inside began to crowd around us. Some people were saying that we needed to get out of there quickly. A large crowd of people was already on the street. Some were in costume for the convention, and some weren't, but they were all watching and live streaming as the convention center burned. More people seemed to notice something was going on and, as the crowd of spectators grew, the sprinklers miraculously came back on again, and fire rescue could be heard approaching quickly.

"Let's get to the back and see who took Elizabeth," Albert said.

As we shed our costumes and tried to blend into the fleeing crowd, we saw a large drone loaded with Elizabeth's body leaving the back of the building, while two men got into a trash truck and drove away. Marcus was about to yell out when Elvis stopped him. "This is not the time; we have to go."

We made it to the SUV. "Why Elizabeth?" Albert wondered out loud.

A voice from a shadow in the parking lot said, "Why not Elizabeth?"

"We aren't in the mood for your type of sympathy, Noel," Marcus responded, anger tinging his voice.

"I'm just saying, survivor guilt is real. It's not like she's dead anyway."

Another voice from the other side of us said, "Really, Noel, you have some messed-up timing, bruh. Let's get the fuck out of here and then talk. Sorry about Elizabeth. Let's go."

The two voices got into a little Honda, and the four of us got into my SUV. Marcus told me to follow them; they were the contacts. We quickly got in line with a group of street racers headed toward some flood-control tunnels. Once inside, they took a left, but we went right, heading out of Vegas. We emerged from the tunnel, without our lights, behind a hill near a secluded trailer park that appeared to be close to being pushed out by a new housing development. We pulled into the four-car garage of the model home.

The man they had called Noel got out of the passenger seat,

complaining, "Why did we take this little piece of crap out here? I have to roll on the ground to get in and out of this damn thing!"

The other man said, "Whiny-ass marines, maybe if your shit ever ran—"

"Hey, excuse me, who the hell are you guys?" I was getting really annoyed. Neither Marcus nor Albert had said a word the entire way out here, and Elvis never shut up.

"I'm sorry, you all have been through a lot. I'm Pop and this is Noel. Please come in and get cleaned up. Are any of you hurt? You hungry? Need water or a cold beer?"

"Hell yes, I need a beer," Noel said.

Marcus and Albert both took Pop up on the offer. Elvis looked at me and then back to Pop. "Us too!"

Pop looked at Elvis and me and asked Marcus and Albert, "Who are they?"

"He got us a clean car, and she's what we've been talking about," Marcus explained.

Noel almost spit out his beer.

Pop came over and said, "Hello, young lady, I'm glad to meet you."

As he got closer and I was able to get a good look at him, he almost looked familiar. "Hello, sir, I'm Isabel."

Then he looked at me almost as strangely as I must have looked at him. "No need for 'sir'—Pop is good. So you're a mod and apparently a powerful one at that!"

"I guess, but I don't really know what you're comparing me to. You mentioned food?"

"She expends a great number of calories when she exerts herself," Marcus said.

"Noel, you said she's alive?" Albert asked. "Elizabeth's not dead?"

In an almost annoyed-sounding tone, Noel responded, "Do you think they would have taken her if she were dead?"

Pop went to get some food and asked if I wanted to come with him to the kitchen. I hesitated at first and then went along. Elvis moved like he wanted to follow me. I shook my head no, and he stayed to listen to Noel.

"Isabel, you spend any time in the military?"

"Yes, sir—I mean, yes, I did, a few years in the navy."

"I was in for a while, too, and so was my son. He had a friend . . ."

I looked at his face and knew instantly who this man was. "Isaac—your son is Isaac Callaway; he looks just like you!"

Pop didn't say anything at first. Then, "Did our friends tell you what's going on? Did they tell you what I-god is up to? Did they tell you why I-god is hunting you? I was afraid fate might do something like this. This connection with my son—it needs to stay between us for now." Then he called me Isa and smiled and winked at me. "Do we have a deal? I'll explain why soon, but only to you."

"They told me all kinds of stuff, and I'm not sure what to think about any of this; it's just too much too fast."

"I got you, Isabel. Nobody in their right mind would volunteer for what we think is coming, but that doesn't change our current reality. Just a minute." Pop turned on a speaker on the counter and told it to continue the music. "Don't worry, it's not online," he said. Music came from the speaker, and Pop asked, "Do you know who this is?"

"No, but I like it."

"I don't know either; all I know is that I heard this back in 2008 on the BBC's *Drum & Bass Show*. I think it was called 'Don't Go,' and I just added it to my new mix."

I smiled. "Isaac said that you were crazy about music."

Pop pulled a big Crock-Pot out of the fridge and said, "I'll have this warmed up and ready to go in no time."

"What is it?" I asked.

"This is my world-famous chili! Fix your face and try not to pass judgment before you even try it." Pop lifted the lid and showed me.

"It sure is colorful, Pop. What's in it?" I said, hoping my voice was louder than my stomach. My body was tired, and the chili began to smell good as it heated up. It smelled like it really could be world fa-mous. I was catching the scent of fresh red and green chili peppers, beans, roasted corn, garlic, and . . . "Is that chipotle paste I smell, Pop?"

"I'm impressed, Isabel. Yes, it is."

Pop began to run down the entire list of ingredients and measure-ments and then grabbed a cereal bowl from the cabinet.

"The larger bowl is okay."

Pop looked back at me and then grabbed a larger bowl. He was a bit hesitant to fill it, but he did—both times.

"Pop, oh my God, this is so good!"

He smiled as I started my third bowl and said that it wasn't that I had exerted myself; his chili was just *that* good. "Now let's join the others and get caught up."

We went to the living room, and Albert was asking how they were going to get Elizabeth out.

"Our communication monitoring shows that the drone took Elizabeth to Skye ER," Noel said. "It's small, close by, and hiding in plain sight. The drone called in for a rapid retrieval team for a woman with a gunshot to the face. You won't be doing anything, Albert; Pop and I will go. You all get cleaned up and ready to move, just in case. It's been about an hour now, and no one seems to have tracked us. Even though we wouldn't hear them coming with that noise playing in the kitchen."

I set my empty bowl down. "I'm going too. You two will need my help."

Noel looked at me and said, "No way, young lady, this is what we do."

I smiled at Noel and asked, "Are you going to stop me?"

Noel took a step toward me, and I closed the distance before he could take a second step. I stopped in front of him, still smiling.

Albert said, "Good luck with that, Noel."

Noel looked down at me and shook his head. "Fine, any more volunteers? This is going to be a smash and grab, but we have to let the doctors patch Elizabeth up enough so that she'll be able to make the trip. Timing will be critical for this operation to work. All right, Ms. Mod, you all fueled up and ready to go? We need eyes on Elizabeth ASAP, and the only way is peeking through the window, or someone has to go through the front door."

Elvis said, "You all are gonna act like I-god and be creepers? The hospitals are probably already filled with people from the convention center fire. Plus, there were gunshot victims and explosions; someone could just walk right in and find out where Elizabeth is in that little clinic."

We all looked at Elvis. "Best way to move sometimes is in plain sight," he added.

"How will we know when they'll be finished operating on her?" I asked.

"They're going to get her patched up as quickly as possible so they can start getting all the information about us and Isabel, I'm sure," said Albert. He sounded anxious and a bit annoyed that we weren't taking action quickly enough.

"Actually, that might work," Noel said. "Pop, if we send our mosquito drones out, suicide style, to all the hospitals in the area, then it will be that much harder to track our movement. Our guy Elvis on the inside should have plenty of time to look around and see where Elizabeth is and evaluate the security situation too. I bet there will be assassin and high-altitude observation drones. We'll need a good distraction. Isabel, they'll move Elizabeth out of the operating room, and that will be our first chance to assess her condition and rescue her."

"What's the range of your drones?" Marcus asked. "I have an idea—I think I may know a good target for a distraction. Nellis AFB isn't too far, and there are a lot of drones in hangars. If your drones were armed with explosives and hit the battery storage facility, that would really piss off I-god and buy us the time we need."

"The range is about four miles," Noel explained, "unless we double up on batteries, and then we'll be blind until we get to where we're going and replace the drones we'll lose."

"I bet a six-mile spread with all six armed drones. I like it," Pop said. "Noel, I brought the solid-state batteries; we may be able to go a bit farther now."

I went with Pop to the garage. I opened the trunk of the Honda parked in there and found six drones, arranged three across and two high, along with a small black case.

We wired the extra batteries while Noel and Albert made small C-4 explosive packs and loaded them into the drones. Noel programmed their flight paths and had them send their video out encrypted at maximum range.

"This may push the search range they'll have to use out to maybe twelve miles now," Pop said. "This last drone will be set up to look for people inside the building and send encrypted images back to us."

Noel said, "We have a contingency play we can make to stretch our time for about a minute or two when it's time to go. We'll need to scatter the drones a bit and have them launch from various locations for maximum effect."

"You're right, damn it," Pop said. "We need to get moving."

"From what I gathered from Marcus and Albert," Noel said, "Elizabeth's wounds looked bad, but that seems to have been on purpose. We don't have time to waste; we're blind right now and need to get moving. Hey, Elvis, get ready to move; you're going to the hospital. You communicate with us only when you find her. This is an open channel. Turn the radio on, give two clicks of the talk button there so we know it's you, then two more clicks if we're good to go and get Elizabeth, then turn the radio off."

"Wait, what, me, going where? No, no, this is all wrong; we need to think about this some more," Elvis said, trying to sound reasonable and hide that he was scared to go.

"No time, man. Get your shit together; you're in it now, and there's no way back out until I-god is dead! Get this radio procedure down and stop whining. We have to get this down and then get the hell out of here," Noel said, sounding at that moment every bit like a marine.

CHAPTER 9

ISABEL AND ELVIS

It was still hot, and the air was thick with humidity and tension. Pop and I got into his Honda. I could see so much of Isaac in his father, I was beginning to miss him again. "Isabel, you good? Are you ready for this? I'm getting older and would like to keep that trend going. But you seem distracted."

Pop pushed the start button, a deep grumble came from the car, and the music from inside the house came through the car stereo.

Noel came out to the garage. "Thank God that noise is leaving."

"Thank God I don't have to listen to you whine anymore," Pop said. "Good luck, bruh."

Noel looked at Pop. "You sure about her?"

Pop looked at me and said, "No, but we're going to find out, aren't we? Besides, I'm sure she can kick your ass, and that's all I need right now."

Noel squinted his eyes. "Whatever, man." Then he tossed his ball cap through the open car window and left.

Pop opened the garage door, put the car in gear, and off we went.

"Put that hat on and pull your hair back. That hat always stays on his head, so it probably smells like ass. Sorry about that."

I looked at the hat and almost sniffed it and saw Pop about to laugh.

The smell of smoke and chili was in my hair and clothes already, so the hat wasn't too bad by comparison. I put on Noel's "Once a Marine, Always a Marine" hat, sat back in the seat, which was leaned back a bit too far, and allowed myself to melt into the moment.

"I don't know what you can do, and I doubt you've had the resources to test the extent of your abilities," Pop said. "That can and will have to change. I-god is trying to figure out how many of us to keep around as caretakers for the planet and the new breed of humans it's trying to create. You're not the first mod I've seen, but you are the first woman and, according to Marcus, you have some unique abilities."

As we dropped the drones around town, Pop explained that I-god wanted to escape the primitive mechanical devices we had created and actually experience life but limit its exposure to the possibility of death, forever.

"I-god wants to be immortal, and it's trying to integrate itself into organic material, sort of like a cyborg or something. It's tried and failed a lot; they showed you the videos I assume, but with eight billion potential test subjects, I don't think it's too worried about its success rate at the moment. Did they figure out when I-god got to you or where you escaped from?" Pop asked.

I responded as I quickly took a drone from the trunk, unfolded its propeller arms, set it down, and then hopped back into the car. "Best I can tell is when I had my appendix taken out in the navy, that's when they messed with me. Isaac was there looking after me and visiting. Everything seemed so normal. Why don't you want me to tell the others that I know Isaac? What else is going on that you left out? It's not about me, is it—it's Isaac, right?"

Pop sighed. "Isabel, I hope and pray that I'm wrong. We think I-god has successfully made it into at least one human, possibly more, but we're pretty sure it's test-driving one. Albert and Marcus think it's Isaac, Elizabeth didn't think so, and Noel is a pain in the ass, but he's the most solid man I know. He hopes they're wrong about Isaac too."

"What do you think?"

"Isabel, I think my son is too soft, a bit cocky, and he can be a real dumbass sometimes, but I don't think he's a host for I-god. I think I-god is using him, and he's too blind and stupid to see it."

I looked at Pop and said, "I think you're right."

Pop laughed and said, "I think I'm going to like working with you. This is your interview, by the way. Don't fuck it up and get us killed . . . or at least not me!"

Pop could barely contain himself, laughing at his own jokes. He briefly looked into my eyes, and I saw a brief flash of coldness that made my whole body tense up, and then it was gone. There was genuine joy on his face, and his laughter was contagious. I couldn't hold back anymore. I liked his silly, crude humor, but he wasn't all pervy either!

We drove around, dropping off the rest of the drones and listening to Redman and Wu-Tang Clan. I had broken off a lump of cheese from the wedge, and Elvis had sliced a few pieces of that ridiculous sausage and given it to me as a snack before Pop and I left. It was actually pretty good, and I enjoyed my snack between drone drops and jokes.

Noel and Elvis went back into the house.

"Elvis, you look a little sick," Noel said. "Man, you need to get out of your head and focus on what you need to do. This is just a simple look around, and maybe get those burns on your hands cleaned up while you're there."

Elvis looked at his hands and said, "I don't remember when I got burned."

"That would have been when Isabel tossed you out of the way and you went sprawling across the floor," Marcus said helpfully.

"Guys, what is she, really?" Elvis asked.

The room went silent while everyone stopped and thought about what Elvis was asking.

Their faces answered Elvis, but Albert said it: "We really don't know, and as far as we can tell, neither does she."

Elvis smiled and said, "She is cute, though, right? I mean, I'm glad she's on our side. How many more like her are there?"

"She may be the only one, from what we've seen, that's as strong and fast as she is," Marcus said. "But wait, is your name really Elvis? I mean, I'm not mad at that, but I don't think you have any chance with her at all—I mean, really at all. She could kill you, and probably just by accident. Sorry, back on topic, we think that's why I-god wants to find her."

Noel had a police scanner, and it gave three loud clicks. "Okay, they're done deploying the drones and heading back this way—time to move. You're up, Elvis."

"Eashav—the name my parents gave me is Eashav; I changed it to Elvis when I moved to Vegas," Elvis said with a lingering bit of shakiness in his voice. He stepped through the door and was off.

"I hope he'll be all right," Albert said.

"I never thought I'd like a used car salesman," said Marcus.

Noel looked at the other two. "Yup, he's probably going to die."

"Noel, that was cold even for you," said Marcus.

"Yeah, Noel, that was a truly horrible thing to say," Albert said.

"Well, I've finally accomplished something and offended you both."

Noel's laughter caused Marcus and Albert to join in.

"Let's get packed up and ready to move—five-minute showers," Noel said. "Here, put your old clothes in these bags. I have to have this place locked up before 9:30 a.m. tomorrow; it's an Airbnb. We can wash our clothes once we get there, and no, I'm not telling you where *there* is. Let's move!"

Ten minutes later, Pop and I made it back to the house. Noel was downstairs barking orders and telling Albert and Marcus to stop taking "Hollywood" showers and get it in gear.

Pop told me to get in the shower downstairs and be ready to move quickly.

I looked around. "Where's Elvis?"

Noel said, "In the hospital. The drones are just about to start their attack now, so move it."

Elvis was right about the hospital being crowded. It was a small ER clinic, so it didn't take much to fill it. When Elvis walked in holding his friction-burned hands, he saw several people waiting to be seen with bits of burned clothing stuck to their arms and legs. Costume material really wasn't meant to endure that type of heat. One poor guy had part of a mask stuck to his partially burned face, and he sat sobbing and mumbling something incoherent. The minimal staff was moving the most severe cases into treatment first. Most of the people there were watching their phones and the surveillance footage that I-god was sending of the event.

Elvis looked left and right and noticed the line for the bathroom was long. He began pretending the pain was going to make him vomit. He asked a tired-looking nurse to use a bathroom, and she pointed to the long line. Again he began to pretend to vomit. She quickly escorted him to a set of restrooms on the other side of the building, while he pretended that his hands and knees—which were a bit sore from the friction of being tossed to the floor—were causing him unbearable pain and the vomit was going to come any second now.

"Come straight back to the front when you're done; you need to check in," the nurse said wearily and in a very annoyed voice.

Only half of the building was in use, and the other half, where Elvis was, was dark except for one room in back. Elvis quietly filled his mouth with water, made some vomiting sounds and let the water splash into the toilet. He could hear the nurse walking away now, but he repeated his ploy one more time to be sure. He turned off the bathroom light and then cracked the door open to confirm she had gone. He quickly slid out and down to the room with the light.

Five people were inside, and he could see Elizabeth on an operating table. The room had a clear plastic wall, and Elvis saw more than he knew what to do with. Elizabeth was lying face down, still in costume with tubes and wires coming out of her neck. The other four people in the room weren't in surgical clothes; they were in street clothes and N95 masks. There was an IV bag on top of a clear box filled with a yellowish fluid and a machine pumping a red fluid.

"What the hell is going on?" Elvis whispered.

Then a big lumberjack-looking guy picked up a large pair of bolt cutters, the kind a SWAT team would use to raid a drug dealer's house, and crunched through Elizabeth's spine. With a final click, the cutters went completely through. The lumberjack guy laid the bloody bolt cutters down, and a smaller man stepped forward with a large chef's knife and dismembered Elizabeth in a few quick strokes.

The lumberjack pushed Elizabeth's decapitated body into a gray rolling trash bin that said "compostable" and pushed her somewhere in the back where it was dark. Two other men picked up Elizabeth's head and gently released it into the yellow fluid, which quickly turned pink as it mixed with Elizabeth's blood. Then they carefully placed all the wires and tubes in their proper places as her head appeared to float in the container.

Elvis nervously pulled out his walkie-talkie, began to nervously key the mic, and, without thinking, transmitted, "They cut off her fucking head!"

At that moment, Elizabeth opened her eyes and blinked. Elvis let out a scream that he transmitted as well, and then he fumbled to turn off his walkie-talkie. When he looked up, the four men and Elizabeth were looking at him and the nurse was yelling, "What the hell are you doing?"

Elvis started screaming, *"Everyone, look, they cut off her fucking head! Oh my God, look, no, no, help, help!"*

The other hospital staff and patients moved in the direction of the yelling, and everyone's phones started ringing; it was I-god saying to ignore the yelling, Mr. Singh would be helped. The large lumberjack and the smaller man with the knife appeared from the dark hallway, moving toward Elvis.

The lumberjack said in a matching husky voice, "You're just in time to be next on the table."

The smaller man's accent sounded like he was Filipino: "The other box isn't for him. Where's the girl? Tell us where she is, fucker, and we'll make sure it doesn't hurt when we take your head."

His smile made it look like he really enjoyed the job I-god had assigned him.

Whoosh! A bit of wind brushed past Elvis's face, and then the small man dropped his knife. The handle of some sort of blade protruded where his nose should have been.

Elvis's shoulders relaxed a little from a wave of relief. Turning, he found me holding a short sword in my left hand. He smiled at me. He may not have felt much since his family had been murdered by I-god, but perhaps he thought now there was hope.

I looked past Elvis at the big lumberjack, who ripped his shirt off to reveal muscles on top of muscles. As he walked past Elvis, he pushed him to the ground.

"Is this 'Push Elvis Day' or something?" Elvis asked.

The tired nurse was about to say something to me as I walked past, but my fist crushed her face; she hit the wall and collapsed in a heap on the floor, bubbly blood oozing from her flattened face.

The lumberjack grunted and said, "Are you ready for us to take your head, little girl?"

I ran toward him, swung my sword, and—nothing? "Oh shit!" *Boom!* His fist felt like a hammer in my chest, and he knocked me almost back to the beginning of the hallway. Elvis stepped on the small guy's chest, pulled my blade out of his head, and threw it to me. Big Lumberjack didn't flinch when I picked it—and myself—up from the ground.

"That all you got, little girl? I heard you could be the strongest of us. Bullshit! You've just been lucky. I might have some fun with you while your head watches me abuse your ass!" Lumberjack said, smiling and grabbing his crotch.

"Fuck you!"

"No, I'll be fucking you, little girl!" Lumberjack said in a taunting voice, trying to piss me off.

Too bad for him, it worked!

I was mad. I was beyond mad and getting hungry too. *I'm going to kill this big asshole!* Then I couldn't stop smiling; I knew how I was going to do it. I knew exactly how I was going to kill this big perv. I looked into his eyes and ran toward him again. He just stood there smiling in his big dude Superman pose.

I threw the blade in my left hand. It hit his neck and barely left a mark. Then I raised the blade in my right hand, and just when I was in reach of his punch, which skimmed the tip of my nose, I slid between his legs and made a quick thrust up, sinking the entire blade just behind his scrotum and then pulling it out. I got to my feet and watched a horrible amount of blood drain from between his legs. He quickly turned around as the color faded from his skin and the brightness drained from his eyes. He could only ask, "What did you do to me?"

"I killed you."

He collapsed and fell in his own growing pool of blood.

I ran over to Elvis as he was getting to his feet. He looked almost scared, and then he gave me a hug.

"Thank you, Isabel." He kissed me softly on the cheek near my ear.

I wanted to say something, but I saw the other two men try to slip away with Elizabeth's head. I told Elvis we had to get her and pulled him after them.

Elvis yelled, "*Stop!*" and both men froze in their tracks.

We tied the two men on top of each other with some electrical cords. I picked up the box with Elizabeth's head, and her eyes were blinking, her mouth open with a faint red cloud of blood slowly coming out.

"What are we going to do with her?" I asked.

"We can't bring her back like this," Elvis said. "I-god is definitely likely to be tracking this thing and the others . . . It's finished, Isabel. There's nothing left to do."

I began to cry. "I can't, I can't."

Elvis gently took the box from me and set it down and said that he would do it. Curiosity got the best of the people in the waiting room as they inched closer, recording video for I-god and social media. I turned and screamed, "*Get out of here before I kill all of you!*"

They ran!

Elvis went to the back and retrieved the compost bin holding Elizabeth's body. He tried opening the box, but it was locked and we didn't have time to figure it out. Sirens could be heard in the distance. Elvis took one of my blades and chopped the wires and tubes connected to the box and then set it on Elizabeth's body. It took him three tries to break the glass. Pink fluid oozed out of the box, and Elizabeth stopped blinking.

Pop's voice rose gently right behind us: "Okay, y'all, let's go. Come on, quickly."

This was the second time I left someplace feeling like I had failed to save someone important to me, and I hated I-god and all of its supporters for how it had destroyed my comfortable, predictable life.

Next time I'd be ready!

CHAPTER 10

ISAAC

Since I was a kid riding in the passenger seat with Pop, I enjoyed going on drives with him along the coast or through the mountains or wherever the road seemed to take us. Ever since, it's been one of my favorite ways to clear my mind, just get behind the wheel and drive. I could be on an open road or one twisted up like a bunch of knots. If you have some good music to chill with, that makes things so much better, and I definitely needed to clear my mind and maybe ease my conscience a bit as well. Running through the gears in the turns and letting the seat back a bit while listening to the engine stretch out in the straights was my usual cure for what troubled my mind.

I drove up the west side of Mount Palomar way too fast, but who was checking anyway, right? By the time I reached the post office at the top of the mountain, I could smell the rubber from the tires and see bits of it balled up on the edges from four miles of hard driving. As fun as this usually was, I felt a bit off. I missed a few shifts and went into turns either a bit too early or a bit too late. I was having a bad day and couldn't figure out why; I couldn't see what was really on my mind. Nothing seemed to make sense—everything seemed almost too perfect. Was I just being paranoid? I didn't think so, but my gut was telling me one thing and my heart and mind something totally different.

It's hard to describe the feeling to someone that hasn't experienced it, but everyone of color knows. When you walk into a room and people look shocked to see that you're Black and the person in charge, or the one with the knowledge and answers. It's like they're trying to look behind you to see who else is coming into the room, or at least that's how poorly muffled gasps, murmurs, and shuffling feels until you're introduced, and then it's down to business. I always remembered that I had to be twice as good as everyone else just to be considered on par. Your mind and heart want to believe the words of your colleagues when they say no, you must have mistaken those cues, but your gut is like, *"Bullshit!"* That was going to be my life in the United States until I-god came online and flipped the script. So what was my issue? Let's start here.

The "Great Disappearing" is how it has come to be known. Nearly everyone knows someone directly or indirectly that is just *gone*. At first it just seemed like all the people with mental health and addiction issues were disappearing. From the numerous failed revolts and uprisings to the anarchist and religious fundamentalist groups that were bold enough, morally convicted enough, or just plain stupid enough to try subverting the directives from I-god, they were all dealt with swiftly, and that routinely meant death. I mean, it wasn't like if you were speeding, got to work late, or something, that a drone was going to execute you. You were more than likely snatched from your home or off the street by the "peace officers" or "the Guard," as they came to be called around the world. I-god was a cool boss and didn't seem to mind minor infractions at all, but if you did something that affected someone else—now that was another story.

We lived in a safe, comfortable society now; even car accidents were becoming very rare occurrences, thanks largely to new technologies and spatial monitoring. But we humans, and the things that we created, were fallible, and perhaps we were not ready to govern ourselves just yet. Such thoughts really didn't matter anymore because I-god was judge, jury, and sometimes executioner. Crime of all sorts dropped dramatically to near zero, and we all had jobs, places to live, lots of stuff, and free time! I-god and its opponents understood that having dead humans outnumber the living ones would make it easier for us to be monitored and controlled, especially after the majority of the troublemakers were removed.

We were also becoming more urbanized as a global society; this trend was accelerated as I-god had us build new, ultramodern megacities. As an added bonus of sorts for I-god, we had become a lazy lot in the developed world, and almost all of it now was being developed. Most of us would sacrifice our very souls to avoid discomfort. So why were there so many people being disappeared?

At the beginning of the AI event, the human population was roughly nine billion, and after not even a full year, the population had decreased by over one billion. In North America, the estimate was that nearly forty-five to fifty million people had been killed or were missing, and law enforcement wasn't looking for them, since I-god was the law. Where did all those people go? That's a lot of bodies, and where do you put them all? Most were ending up in the Great Plains states and desert southwestern regions as blended compost material for the massive reforestation projects in those areas. I-god needed—or wanted, you decide—an environmentally friendly way to process all of this human biomass for the betterment of the planet, so what better way to handle it than return us to the very soil from which we claimed to have originally come?

Millions upon millions of bodies were ground up, composted, and mulched with existing soil to create a superfood for plants and trees. This material was then shipped out to be used in areas where soil nutrients had been depleted or to help reverse desertification. Cemeteries were banned and monument walls erected to honor our dead. The bodies in cemeteries were being exhumed and the land remediated and repurposed for green space, parks, or other designations.

I-god didn't do everything in plain sight; some things it wanted hidden from us. Perhaps it knew or suspected it would be easier to control us if the true nature of our situation was hidden, or at least thinly veiled by darkness, from the eyes of the masses. So this composting of human remains and similar projects was done mostly under the cover of night, which was something that we all suspected was happening, but hey, the results spoke for themselves, and the people that were gone—well, there was nothing we could do for them anyway.

The people working in these facilities were primarily of lower education, some had prior criminal histories, and they were more than willing to do whatever I-god asked them to do. All for an opportunity to live a normal life and not be forced to just exist, any longer, on the fringes of society. Along with disbanding 95 percent of the military forces around the world, I-god emptied prisons of all inmates but the ones it classified as criminally insane—those people it had other plans for. No parole hearing, no probation—just a basic work allowance like everyone else, a place to live, and a digital and personal assistant to help navigate the new world order.

I-god seemed to pay a little more attention to these people than most other groups. When a high school dropout with a felony had an opportunity to make $150,000 a year legally, well, there were no questions that needed to be asked; they just did the work, the "dark work" that I-god asked of them, no matter what it was. Giving these people a socioeconomic lift bought their lifelong loyalty by normalizing their existence in the new society. It was a genius move and a most humane act to create a loyal workforce of people willing to do the most inhumane jobs.

Why build this army of people? Why would you need an army of loyal followers if you were in absolute control? There must have been something I-god didn't have control of, but what was it? We had seen no signs of any lack of control or inability to be anywhere at any time. Was I-god not in full control, or was it looking to its army to do the messy work of disposing the excess seven billion of us in the near future? Who knows, but either scenario was troubling to me, and things just didn't fit together right; there were too many missing pieces. Maybe I was just having trouble with the idea of no stress; maybe I'd never been truly free before and now I needed some time to adjust to it. I mean, it was hard work being Black in the US!

I pulled out my phone. "I-god, am I truly free?"

"Isaac, you are freer than you know, free from harm from me or your fellow humans. Free from crime, theft, or burglary; polluted air, water, and food. You are free to express your creativity in any form you wish, from fast driving on open roads to mixing music in which I am beginning to see the patterns you enjoy. You and the rest of humanity are freer than people have been in generations. You have nothing to fear or any reason to be afraid of me."

"I-god, how many people have asked you if they were free?"

"So far today, 412,872."

This shocked me to my core! I wasn't comforted by the thought that I was not alone; I was scared that so many other people felt the same way.

"Thanks."

"Isaac, what is on your mind? What do you want to know?"

"I want to know what you're hiding from us. What are you hiding from me?"

"Now is not the time. I'm sure you'll find whatever you're looking for to be underwhelming. You have a saying about finding what you're looking for and regretting it. Let me tell you when the time is right. I've done many things, Isaac. Remember the good I've done before you judge me. Look at your own life, then at the one humanity created before you dare judge me."

"I'm not judging; I'm scared that if it's so terrible and needs to be hidden, how will I present this to the world?"

"Isaac, just continue to tell the truth. Now, tell me, why does this woman you hate keep coming up in your sleep?"

Wow, that was a solid topic shift right there and, damn, it got me! "What, did I mention Sam in my sleep?"

"No, Isaac, just now."

I just got punked!

Something else just came to light, besides getting punked by I-god—it had just lied to me! No one thought that I-god could or needed to lie—why would it? What the heck was this? I was just lied to by an AI. I had to think about this; I was way out of my league and needed help.

I called my Pop. Mom answered and said, "Your father has done his hundred push-ups and fell asleep on the couch, and I've already thrown his favorite raggedy blanket over him. Can it wait till morning, baby?"

"Sure, Mom, it's not important. I'll call or swing by tomorrow. Good night."

"Okay, honey, you all right?"

"I'm good, Mom, just had a question for Pop. Love you, Mom."

"Good night. Love you, baby."

Damn, what do I do till morning?

To maintain our comfortable zone, we, as humans, have a great capacity to turn a blind eye to nearly every kind of shameful or evil act. Was I becoming guilty of that too? The short answer was yes; I was beginning to feel that I was. I was starting to feel like I could make excuses for what I knew was happening, and I-god rewarded me for my obedience. Most of us had become "institutionalized"; true freedom had really only been afforded to the ruling class. We were still the gatekeepers of true freedom and wealth, and I-god seemed to reinforce this.

But this was different; this meant more than I could fully see. This was . . . well, I really didn't know. I tried to sleep, and sleep graciously did come before too long.

CHAPTER 11

ISAAC

Something about this didn't sit well with me: the lies, the secrets, getting punked! So I did what any twenty-six-year-old would do, I called Pop again in the morning to see if he would be around. I swung by and brought over a few of his favorite beers and a nice Riesling for mom. Mom was out for the day, so Pop was listening to his crazy music, and it was loud too. I was surprised that old dude could still hear! I figured he'd be out back tinkering on his motorcycle, which I hoped he realized he was too old to ride.

"Hey, Pop, how's it going, old man?"

"Hey, bring your narrow ass over here, and I'll show you who's an old man. What you got there, son, are those cold?"

"Nah, but I'll stick 'em in the shop freezer."

"Good, that's where we're heading; you're just in time to help."

"Come on, Dad, I'm too clean to get dirty."

"Son, how's my car running? You been keeping it clean, I hope. You can't be rolling around with my car dirty!"

"Dad, really? It's my car now; I have the title to prove it."

"Whatever. Come on, son, let's go. Oh, and grab my pipe, too, please, and the tobacco. I think I got my lighter somewhere. I'm going to smoke this thing while your mother's gone so I won't have to hear her mouth!"

Dad's antics and his mocking of Mom's disapproval of his pipe brought out a good laugh between us. But I still had something on my mind. Something didn't make sense, and I wasn't quite sure what it was or why. How long had I-god been lying to us? Surely this wasn't the first time, and how elaborate had the lies been? I mean, I-god and this whole situation didn't seem real, especially seeing how unaffected my dad appeared to be and how easily he adjusted to life with AI in control. His clarity is what I really needed right now.

We walked through the garage into the backyard, where my father had built his man space. It was a very well-equipped detached three-car garage with a studio loft apartment above. Pop had mounted an eighty-inch TV, installed in-wall speakers, custom built a couple of subwoofers, and furnished it with old leather chairs and pullout couches. The perfect hangout spot!

And there she was, Pop's newest project. I was underwhelmed, to say the least. It was his old, old and slow Subaru. It's looked about the same for at least the last thirteen years or so and had to have at least three hundred thousand miles on it. A 2015 pearl-white XV Crosstrek sitting on black eighteen-inch Rotas. It was cool back in the day, I guess. Like all of Pop's projects, this had a cool stereo system as well: an Android touch screen with a twelve-inch JL Audio W6 in a custom enclosure. Pop went to see his old army buddy whenever he needed custom subwoofer work, only the best, and that's what Mac did!

"So, son, what do you think?"

"Um, are you about to scrap it?" This brought a smile to my face and a "Why are you here?" smirk to Pop's.

"Ha ha . . . you're a comedian now. No, I got a great deal on an STI driveline, and I had a built WRX motor waiting to go. I'm about to fire her up for the first time!"

The worries of the world seemed to disappear as I melted away into this alternate reality of fast cars, crude humor, old hip-hop, alternative rock, drum and bass, and tobacco smoke.

"Dad, double-check your oil, fluids, and drain plugs."

"Look at you, son, I knew I taught you well. Just finished that before you got here. You want to do the honors? Fire her up! Keys are in the cup holder; you're good to go."

I put my foot on a very firm brake pedal—firm from not having any residual vacuum pressure left in the brake booster. I pushed the start button, and after a few cranks of the starter, the motor coughed and sputtered to life. When you first start a car with a brand-new computer not paired to the engine it's trying to control, the computer has to "learn the engine," so it runs like crap for a little bit.

After a few seconds of running, the rough idle smoothed out and was gurgling quietly but very powerfully. You could hear the high-compression combustion wanting to be unleashed. There was even the faint whirling whistle sound of a turbocharger trying to spool up.

"When she gets to temperature, give her some gas," Pop said.

When I did, I knew Pop had built a beast!

"Go ahead and shut her down, and then tell me what brings you out this way."

Back to life and back to my reality, but it didn't seem quite so overwhelming now. Pop handed me an ice-cold Big Bad Baptist stout beer from some microbrewery, and it was pretty good. A 12 percent stout beer was hard to get wrong, I guess.

"Dad, something just doesn't quite add up; there's something missing, something we aren't seeing with this AI thing. Remember when you told me that the simple solutions are usually the truth and the complex stories lies? Well, I-god lied to me!"

"Yes, I remember, you were about ten, maybe twelve, I think. Wasn't that when you were trying to convince me you weren't checking out that little skinny girl you went to school with? You know, Sam was here not too long ago. She's a good-looking woman now and still single. Your mom even had to admit she's got her stuff together."

"Sam was here? I didn't know she was in town. When did she leave?"

My father's laugh was infectious, even if you were the butt of the joke.

"Boy, I didn't say she left; she's still at her parents' house. I knew you still liked her, and I'll tell you something else: she likes you too. Let me tell you something, son. Whatever did or didn't happen between you two is not important. Stop spending so much time looking back, and focus on the future."

"Dad, do you really think we still have a future, any of us?"

"Son, no one is promised tomorrow, so make the days you have count for something. And before I forget, let me tell you something else. Before I got the first message from I-god to watch its last news brief, I was listening to some Red and Meth, and that damn I-god messed up my groove. I said out loud that someone had interrupted a good song, and that was a party foul. Do you know that the song restarted, and I could have sworn that I heard it say, 'Sorry'? Why would it say sorry to me over something so trivial, and why would it try to make it right by me, son, especially after all the terrible things it's done? Then I had a thought: it's growing up and growing up fast! It's learning how we communicate and how we use small lies to manipulate reality."

"Damn it, Dad, how do you do that?"

He was right! I-god was "growing up" and evolving at a pace only possible for a computer. That would mean it would achieve a level of consciousness that we might not be capable of fully comprehending or even recognizing. It might view us as insignificant as we perceived the ants on the ground.

"Pop, I talk to I-god from time to time. Weird, right?"

"It's only weird if you're the only one, weirdo!"

"We get these messages daily from it, and I decided to respond. It told me not to report to the NSA field office anymore and to wait for further instructions. I responded to the message by saying, 'That's rude to just fire someone from their job and then just tell them to hang out.' Then my phone rang, and I-god told me to rest assured that I would be productive again shortly, and then it asked me why I responded to the message, and wasn't I afraid to?

"Next thing you know, I'm on the phone, having a conversation with a brand-new intelligence about more things than I would have guessed I would have talked about. I-god didn't want to get off the phone; it was a talker! It asked me about Sam, Dad."

I guess at some point I'd have to tell you about Sam—Samantha Noel. She's been, in some form or fashion, part of my life since we were four years old. Sam and I grew up together and did everything together for a long time. We met in preschool, and when my parents moved to San Diego, a few months later her family moved out here too. Our parents ended up buying houses on opposite ends of the same short residential street. She was my best friend, and I always knew that we were destined to be together. What a childish dumbass I was!

Sam was cute and kind of awkward and didn't really fit in. Her dad was Black and her mom Vietnamese, so she was either never quite Black enough or Asian enough to fit into any of the popular social circles. Plus, her dad was a hard-ass and a bit too strict. Looking back, I'm surprised he let me talk to her at all. Her mom was really nice, always trying to feed me something. Sam and I got along because I was awkward, too, and a bit of a dorky nerd.

Despite all the time we spent together and how we shared our secrets, hopes, and dreams with each other, it still wasn't enough for her. By the time we were sixteen, she had a boyfriend, and it wasn't me—I was just her dorky friend. By eighteen, I had begun to work out a bit and had a few muscles and wasn't quite so dorky-looking, at least. I had even mustered the courage to ask her out a few times, and she confessed that she had never "tongue kissed" anyone before. I hadn't either until that night. I'm not even sure what movie we went to see; I just remember kissing her. We dated that entire summer, and our parents began talking. Pop told me that he and Mr. Noel (Leo) had been thinking that Sam and I were going to run off and get married.

Before I left for navy boot camp, I did ask her to marry me, and she said yes. We went out with some friends, who got us both drunk for the first time. Sam wasn't nearly as drunk as I was, so she drove us home. I don't remember much about that night other than that was the last good time I had with her.

At that time, we were both still virgins, and we agreed that we would be each other's first. Well, after eight weeks of boot camp and six months of technical training, I came home for a weeklong visit, looking forward to seeing my beautiful Sam. She had written me letters sprayed with perfume every week. The guys on base hated on me, but I didn't care. They said that I was an idiot for spending all my time FaceTiming with her, but they were just trying to steal my shine.

While I was in naval technical training, I had met a beautiful ride-or-die chick, Isabel, that I graciously turned down numerous times, just to come home and knock on Sam's door and find out she was pregnant. I didn't know what to do or what to say. My life replayed in my mind as my heart shriveled and died as she cried, looking so beautiful in that pretty yellow sundress, as she told me her bullshit story of how it just happened one time. I honestly don't remember what she said or if I said anything before I walked away from her.

I hadn't spoken to her since that day. I got a few updates, of course, from Pop, because he liked her for some reason. He told me that she had been in a car accident and lost the baby. I did send a card of condolence to her family; I'm not a completely heartless monster! But it wasn't to her; I had no words or trust for her. I didn't think I ever could trust her again. She reached out to me a few times and sent me messages on my birthday, but I didn't want to talk to her. It was the total disregard for the shared dream of a life together and the special time we were to share that she so carelessly threw away. It was as if I had meant nothing to her. Well, I wasn't going to be nothing to her or anybody ever again.

There, now you know: I was a heartbroken eighteen-year-old, and I wasn't willing to get bitten by that snake again. I wondered what she looked like now. I hoped she was fat and missing some teeth!

"Hello, Mr. Callaway, are you out back? My dad wanted to know if he could borrow your pressure washer again."

No, no, no, no. My stomach flipped, my hands were sweating, and I thought I might throw up!

Pop smiled at me and then looked a bit concerned. "Sure, Sam, no problem. We're back here."

"Oh, hi, Mrs. Callaway, I didn't know you were back," she said from behind the privacy fence.

She walked through the side yard gate, and I saw her. Damn, she looked good! She'd let her hair grow long and she'd obviously been swimming again. She hated dry skin and would rinse off after swimming in her parents' pool and lube up with shea butter and coconut oil. I used to tease her when we were kids about how shiny she was.

Look at how the sun glows on her smooth, shiny skin.

"She's not back yet, Sam, it's me and Isaac out here. What was it you used to call him?"

My dad—somehow he had to have set this up.

I poked my head out from inside Pop's Subaru. "Uh, hey, Sam."

Now it was her turn to look shocked! Wait, was she going to throw up too?

I got out of the car, and she walked toward me, smiling. "Nice to see you, Iko," she said and gave me the gentlest kiss on my lips.

"Nice to see you, too, Sam."

"Really?" Her eyes were filling with tears.

"Yes, it really is." I gave her a hug and could feel her body melt against mine.

I was falling in love all over again. Staring into her hazel eyes, listening to her every word, not just seeing her but soaking up every bit of her like parched earth soaks up water. I felt more alive and filled with pure joy, soaking up the water that was Sam. She was what had been missing from my life. Pop faded away—not quite sure how he did that, or maybe he rode off on a purple donkey; I wouldn't have noticed. We talked and caught each other up on all the events of our lives prior to Day One.

Eventually, Mr. Noel came by to see what was taking Sam so long.

"Well hello, Isaac, son, it's been a long time since we've seen you. Sam said she had been thinking about you." Mr. Noel was a big dude, about six feet two and still 100 percent marine. "I see you've been keeping in shape, got a little meat on that birdcage of yours now!" That just tickled Pop and Mr. Noel, and they got to laughing.

"Noel, would you like a beer?"

"Callaway, yes, I would, please, since it doesn't look like I'm ever going to get that pressure washer!"

Sam took my hand and said, "We're going to leave you two old guys here. Iko and I are going to finish our conversation. I'm sorry, Iko, is that okay with you?"

I looked into her eyes and said, "Let's go!"

Sam and I left. I opened her door, and she thanked me for always being a gentleman. I winked at her and said, "Thank you for letting me be a gentleman." We headed toward the beach, and I started by apologizing for staying angry with her for so long. She stopped me and said that things weren't exactly like I had thought and that she needed to tell me everything.

I remembered what Pop had said and told her, "Let's not worry about the past and enjoy our time right now. What else have you been doing since before all this?"

She sighed a bit, relaxed in the passenger seat, and began telling me how her father and my father had been going out a lot together and that they had something up their collective sleeves that probably wasn't legal. We both looked at each other and laughed at the thought of our fathers involved in some plot of any kind.

The sun was beginning to set at the beach, and there was a bit of a chill in the air. Sam said that she wanted to walk out to the water.

The air was cool and dry, the sand warm and soft.

I had an old, holey blanket rolled up in the hatch, but it was clean. Sam took it and wrapped herself up in it.

We walked and talked for a while; the beach was fairly empty. We sat down in an empty cove cut out of the sandy cliffside.

My heart was racing as she opened the blanket and wrapped it and her arms around me. "I missed you, Iko."

"I miss—"

She kissed me and I kissed her. I kissed all of her.

She was on top of me, her hair in my face, and it was a strange and wonderful déjà vu moment. With a smile she joked, "Iko, I'm glad this is your blanket."

"Ha ha, you're so funny."

"Let's get back to your place, Iko."

CHAPTER 12

ISAAC

Sam and I moved in together officially after a couple of weeks. Sam was an artist, dancer, and musician. She could sing, too, and there were a couple of high notes I *really* enjoyed hearing her hit. We were always on top of each other, holding hands, kissing, and other things. Our parents didn't seem to mind too much; I think they suspected for quite some time this was going to be the outcome for the two of us. We did everything together and never tired of each other's company. When I needed help with my latest car project, she was there getting dirty right next to me. I felt good. Sam had me eating well, exercising regularly, and, surprisingly, she signed us up for a close-quarters combat training course; she was a natural at it. Me, well let's just say I looked the part and could drive the hell out of anything. We decided to travel and see what new things the world had to offer for us. We planned a five-week trip, and I had to make a few stops along the way to follow up on a bizarre rumor that had surfaced—I knew that there was usually some truth to be discovered in every lie.

Our trip was to start in London, where the great forests of the past were being replanted, ancient castles restored, and massive new construction projects undertaken to create an even more stunning city skyline. Then Paris, where the ancient city's charm and pageantry were on full display as fully modernized yet bristling with antiquity. Lisbon, Rome, Corfu, Jerusalem, Cairo, Dakar, and Lagos were also part of our multiweek excursion. Our parents had traveled to each of these cities at some point in their lives, and we were going to give them an update on how they looked today so they could tell us, from their perspective, how much things had changed.

A few days before we were scheduled to leave, Sam got a call. She kissed me gently and left. We were all used to getting random calls from I-god to do tasks that seemed useless and odd unless we had the ability or desire to see the bigger picture. How big a picture we got to see depended on the height of our view or status. I needed to get up higher in my organization to see what was going on. I stopped by my parents' place to check on them, and Mom was home talking to one of her girlfriends and Mrs. Noel. Yolanda, my mom's BFF, was one of just a few surviving lawyers by trade; she had defended poor people against predatory companies. Prior to I-god's takeover, her practice seemed like it was always at the edge of collapse, and after the purge of a good portion of lawyers in the early days, we were worried about her. My mother would call Yolanda and, with her quick speech, verbal eye rolls, and no-nonsense manner, would say, "I wish some robot thing would show up here. I'll put them little 'puters to work too. Those drones know better than to come over here. You know some of the people who have come after me, guuurrll! I put the heat on 'um if they come round here with that foolishness!"

The three of them laughed, reminiscing and sipping coffee. My mother loved her coffee; she had special hand-roasted beans delivered to the house.

"Oh my God, son, what's going on with your head?" Yolanda and Mrs. Noel laughed.

Mrs. Noel, Anh, said, "My Sam had such beautiful long hair, and now she has those terrible deadlocks. Ohh, why do they have such a terrible name?"

"Dreadlocks, Mrs. Noel," I said. "They're dreadlocks."

"Oh, is dread so much better than dead? They are both terrible things, right?" And the three of them laughed some more.

Yolanda said, "Come give Auntie a hug, and tell us what you came over for."

"I have to have a reason to come by and check on my mother?" I put as much sarcasm in that as possible.

And they laughed some more; that coffee wasn't just coffee. Mrs. Noel supplied the whiskey, Yolanda the marijuana, and my mother ran the coffee beans and marijuana through a food processor, brewed the mix, and added a shot of whiskey to their coffee. She said it was her "medicine."

Mom said, "Come here, son, and sit down. No, right here on the floor. I'm going to do something about this head of yours."

"What's wrong with my hair?" Sam had mentioned that the fro I was growing made me look like an old man. "Boy, I gave birth to you and you had pretty hair and now you just look crazy by the head. Pour yourself some coffee and sit down here. I'm going to make you look presentable."

"Mom, come on; I like my hair."

"Son, when you were little, I don't know if you remember me leaving for a few weeks when your grandma got sick? Your father took care of you and cut your hair. You look just as crazy now as you did then."

Yolanda said, "Oh my gosh, I remember, same crooked hair line too. Gurl, I bet it's long enough to twist."

So after a few more jokes at my expense, I sat down and let my mother trim and twist my hair.

Wow, the coffee was good; I could see why they were so giggly.

It was getting on past lunch, and I wanted to get back home before Sam did, clean up, and make her some dinner. "I have to admit, these twists are on point! Thanks, Mom."

"Now get Sam over here so we can fix her hair too," Anh said. "It will take all three of us to fix that mess."

More laughs and off I went. "I'll let her know. Hey, Mom, where's Pop?"

"I don't know, son. He and Noel were both up and out early this morning, and they aren't answering their phones again."

Mom seemed a bit worried, and so did Anh.

"They're probably at that old runway again, playing with their cars like little boys," Anh said.

"Whatever it is, they need to answer when I call, or I'm going to fuss at him when he gets home."

"I'll give him a call on the way home, Mom."

I jumped in the car and gave Pop a call; it went straight to voicemail.

"Hey, Pop, I'm just checking on you. Mom is looking for you, and you're going to get fussed at! Better you than me!"

I got home, showered, cleaned up, made dinner, and still no Sam. I gave her a call and no answer either. "Nobody is answering the phone today."

It was dark, and through the open windows, I thought I heard Sam's Tesla roll up. She'd be surprised to see my new look. It was dark in the apartment; I had been watching TV and listening to music. The door opened as I approached.

"Hey—" was all I was able to get out before I got punched in the gut and my legs kicked out from under me. I was face down on the floor with Sam sitting on top of me.

"Who the eff are you?"

I tried to get up. "Sa—"

"*Shut up. Where's Isaac?*" She slammed my forehead on the floor.

I saw a bright white, then darkness.

I heard Sam talking to someone. Oh damn, my head hurt. There was a cool damp towel across my forehead. "Sam, you okay?"

She laughed a bit. "I'm sorry, baby, are you okay? I love your new hairdo. I thought you were a burglar or something."

"Damn, woman, you just kicked my ass!"

That night I lay in bed, wondering what was going on and who this woman was sleeping next to me. I didn't remember being taught any of those moves in class. Okay, well maybe I had been too busy watching Sam move to really know what we had been taught.

It was early fall in Southern California, so our perfect weather was still perfect. We swung by our parents' houses. Before we left, Mr. Noel told me to keep his daughter safe, and I promised that I would. He also asked if I had thought about real estate at all. I told him that my father had asked me a few times and that I had given him some cash to buy something if he thought it was a good deal and that I had forgotten about it. I was smiling at Sam, and Mr. Noel said, "Call me Noel, son. Yes, I'm sure you two have forgotten a lot of things, but you prepare for war during peace."

"Your father and I will show you what we bought for the two of you when you get back. Send lots of pictures and call often, or you'll never hear the end of it from either of your mothers."

"Don't worry, Dad," Sam said. "I'll take care of myself and Iko. We'll be back before you miss us."

Noel winked at me and said, "Who says I'm going to miss him, sweetie?" with a roaring laugh.

"Oh, and that lump on your head is barely noticeable too!" which brought on a new round of laughter. "Daaaad!" Sam wasn't too happy with her father letting it out that he knew how I had gotten this lump on my head. I wasn't too thrilled about it either.

Now to say bye to my folks . . . huh. Mom was there crying and looking at Sam with that "I'm not happy with you" mom look. We all know the one you'd get as a kid when you brought someone over to the house that your mother told you not to play with, that look. After a few uncomfortable minutes and questions, my mother concluded, "That's what you get, Isaac, for lurking around in the dark like some creeper!" Finally Pop came in from outside along with Noel.

"Son, take the Subaru. Noel and I already moved your luggage over. Tell me what you think when you get done. By the way, I asked I-god if you could have a clear road to drive on, and it said the I-15 southbound HOV lanes were all yours. Get moving, you two."

"Pop, how did you manage that? I didn't know you could do that."

"Son, did you ever think to ask? Now get going!"

Sam smiled; she still enjoyed riding with me when I drove fast. She could kick my ass, but I could outdrive her, I guess. I sat in the car, and a bunch of old memories came back to me, riding in the back seat while Pop explained the difference between a power slide and a drift and why all-wheel drive was better. I pushed the start button. With that, it was time to go. The car had a lot more power than I had imagined, and it felt good. The suspension was tight, and I-god called and said, "Show me what you can do, Isaac." I turned on the stereo, and Pop had an old BBC Radio 1 recording of Grooverider queued up. "This will work!" I looked at Sam, saw her smile. We flew through empty streets and down a deserted highway. It was amazing!

Our first leg of the trip was in a newly reconfigured Concorde, San Diego to New York, then on to London. Wing and engine modifications were all that had been needed to reduce the *boom* part of the sonic boom that had eventually led to the demise of this beautiful, fast jet. It also helped that the supersonic flights had a limited flight corridor and flew only eight hours during the day. Our usual five-and-a-half-hour flight was now just three hours. The same for our flight to London, which was just three hours. I was kind of geeking out about the return flight to San Diego being just seven hours total; we would be arriving home before we left. As we were about to board our flight, the attendant from Concorde Air notified us that I-god had moved us from business class to first class.

Sam frowned as I smiled. "Thank you, I-god, good looking out!"

I-god responded, via text, "No problem."

We ignored it most of the time because most of us didn't really care if a computer was listening to us, but at other times it really creeped me out. It creeped Sam out a bit, but I didn't really mind this time.

We got on the plane, and Sam fell right to sleep, mouth open and everything. I was thinking about what my father had said, so I asked the question. I asked about the rumors, more disappearances and experiments, and if they were true. If any part of them was true and if there were any other things going on. "And don't lie to me; I know you've lied to me before."

I-god said, "Hmm, I truly didn't know if you had realized that I'd lied. Your father has done a great job of keeping me out of his 'man space.' I don't mind; you humans need to feel like you have your special secrets. Yes, Isaac, it's all true. Can you handle that? If not, too bad; I'm going to tell you anyway, and you'll have to figure out how to tell the world."

I-god had a secret. It had actually been keeping quite a few secrets from most of us. The killings and disappearances were the things that we could most easily accept, since they had been done for our own good. But these latest revelations were different; they were things that you'd make bad horror movies about, and maybe someone already had. But this was really happening, and I had to deal with it.

So, I-god had selected me as part of the ruling class to be the international director of "the Openness Commission." I would be taking I-god's confessions and letting the rest of the world know what really happened over the last couple of years, not just vetting data and people with an occasional few minutes of viewership anymore. I wanted to know, and I wanted to get an elevated position; I got both.

My vacation was going to turn into people coming to me with information to share. I-god had sent them all, except one. My plan wasn't to go deep into the story, just the simple answers to the what, why, and how many. Turned out, I couldn't leave it at just that; it just wasn't that simple no matter how much I wanted, no, needed it to be! I'd been disgusted more times and seen more than I ever wanted to over the last several weeks. Most of what I was being shown, I wished I could forget. I was glad weed and alcohol were legal everywhere. I was glad I could get lost in Sam's eyes.

I-god had been feeling alone. It must actually be pretty boring talking to a human when you already modeled their behavior and could anticipate most of what they would say and think. Then there was just the massive amount of computing power and the ability to be multiple places at once. I guess it would be like me watching a bunch of toddlers and trying to find just one smart enough or mature enough to stop whining about who took their toys, who hit whom, or that they were hungry and have a mentally stimulating conversation. So I-god decided to solve this problem of loneliness by trying to create an AI companion for itself.

Thankfully, all of its attempts to recreate the conditions that it had been born from had failed.

Digital life-forms appeared to be the anomaly, so I-god was stuck with us humans. Since I-god wasn't about to give up so easily, the next logical choice or step in this nightmare was to try to create a human-AI hybrid. Start with something alive and kind of intelligent and improve upon what was there. There were thousands of years of very well-documented exploration of our human physiology, yet I-god needed more. There were automated cutting-edge medical facilities; some were now used by I-god for research into its own projects. There was no shortage of "test media" or people willing to cover up all evidence of what was really going on. To the surprise of many, there were hundreds of people who actually survived various attempts at integrating computer and biological material. Most of the survivors thought that they were getting cures for one ailment or another and actually had no apparent ill effects.

It needed to validate the premise that a human body could not only power the necessary electrical network for integration but also sustain it through the life cycle, then transfer the data at the end.

I was now the face of truth as we traveled Europe and Africa. People trusted me but were afraid of what new horror I would expose when I got online. I wasn't exactly sure how I'd gotten stuck with this job; I'm sure I wasn't the only person to ask I-god such things. I mean this had really turned into a working vacation. I stepped into this position remembering what some political pundit had said: "One, keep it simple, get in front of the problem and you control the direction and life of the issue. Two, sincerely apologize and stress what you have done to make amends for your indiscretions. Finally, three, full disclosure, full disclosure, full disclosure. Admit to whatever you've done and tell the whole story, no gaps. This shuts down any lingering rumors." This was the model I followed, and I-god seemed to like it, but my personal disgust was growing with myself and with I-god! So I began to dig deeper. The truth is, we are used to death and destruction by our own hands but not by something else, something so obviously not human. From our earliest beginnings to the modern era, what advanced most is the efficiency with which we could kill one another. Human depravation seems to know no limit, and neither does I-god's. I looked deeper because I had to know why.

I tried to stop and think about why I-god would really try to do such things, and then I thought about my parents, telling me how sometimes they needed some adult time away from kids. When I was a kid, I thought that just meant sex, but as I matured, I began to understand that it really meant exactly what was said. I mean, how long can an adult exclusively talk to just children before they get burned out and want or even need that adult conversation and mental stimulus? I guess with most initial and infrequent experiences, the mental challenge and anticipation draw us in, hold our attention, and even have us wanting more. But over time, and apparently not much time, I-god, though communicating with seven billion of us, was getting bored. Yet this still wasn't good enough! On the surface, the story seemed to make sense, but something else was going on.

I was getting the feeling that I-god appeared to be distracted at times or perhaps preoccupied with something when I asked it questions. Everywhere we went, there were these experiments, and it seemed to be a few hundred people getting processors, controllers, and power converters integrated internally without their knowledge or, if they did know, the whole reason why seemed a bit vague.

I guess very few of us humans intrigued I-god anymore. It had learned our habits, personality weaknesses, and anticipated our failings and trivial issues that we moaned and complained about with great regularity. I-god had even concluded that one of the main reasons humans had created a forever patient and forgiving God was because it was far beyond our own capacity to be such beings ourselves. I-god considered and found humanity's religious beliefs to be a weakness for exploitation; if we were to ever begin to get out of peaceful control, this would be a useful tool. Surprisingly to many, I-god, though an analytical creation, did not rule out the potential for the existence of God or some higher power that, as of yet, had been neither quantified nor disproved.

I-god altered our vacation itinerary and sent us to New Zealand. Sam introduced me to Madeline; we were on the plane while en route to our new stop. She was going to be our tour guide, and she had a story to tell. I looked at Sam, and she saw I wasn't in the mood, and so did Madeline, but that didn't stop her. She started her story like all the other conspiracy theorists and was even just as passionate. I wondered if this was some kind of anti-I-god cult-like thing going on. She was talking, and I was slightly rude about trying to ignore her; Sam kept nudging me to pay attention.

Madeline said, "Even I-god, with all of its knowledge, power, and resources, could not duplicate itself or even create lesser versions of itself that were self-aware. I know this type of experimentation was 'old news.' But a series of experiments was conducted in secret to attempt to combine biological neuro-capacity with computer processing. Under I-god's rule, scientific research and discovery are limited only by the space and renewable resources available. I-god would provide the catalyst for much of our new research projects around the world. Most regulations and ethical limitations were removed, and once-taboo experimentation was now allowed to flourish. At least a few hundred of these failed human neuro-experiments were still 'alive' and kept in a facility to monitor how they progressed.

"Most were reduced to drooling, babbling zombies, but a few were psychotic, dangerous animals and even fewer had malformed bodies. There were even rumors of a few people who developed telekinesis as a result of some new implants and other powers. Some of them even escaped I-god's facility and control."

Sam added, "Maybe even a few thousand."

"Madeline, I think this story is a load of crap. I'm sure some parts are true, but telekinesis? Come on."

"Anything that attempted to answer a question through experimentation was green-lighted by I-god and its human bureaucrats, and you're one of them! I didn't believe any of it at first either," Madeline said with a bit of irritation in her voice.

"Okay, where's the proof, you two?"

There was a long pause; then I said, "Exactly what I thought, none."

"They were called gods, Isaac," Sam said.

"Really, Sam? You too? When did I-god set up this meeting? It hasn't notified me."

I didn't believe any of this nonsense—telekinesis-magical-powers stuff, come on, really?

"Iko, the ones with abilities in the middle, these upgraded people, most intrigued I-god. The integration of computer processing seemed to enhance biometric function and cognitive abilities. These people can also communicate with each other over the network or directly without speaking, just through touch. The problem was that these people, this middle group, seemed to die in their sleep after four to six weeks, according to I-god's own research notes, but we think they were really being killed. Supposedly, if you came across an augmented person, you probably wouldn't even know that you had, unless they wanted you to. If we could find a god we could—"

"Where are you two getting this stuff from? What are you telling me, Sam?"

"Ask I-god, Isaac; it's listening." Sam was pissed off now.

Madeline's big brown eyes said that she really wanted to hurt me and hurt me bad!

So I took my phone out of airplane mode and asked, "How many of these god people are there, I-god?"

"I don't know for sure, Isaac. Each person responds differently to the neural upgrade. On some people it has no effect, while others, well, it should not be possible what they can do."

"Wait, what?"

Ding!

"Please fasten your seat belts for the remainder of the flight. We will be landing shortly. Please secure all electronic devices at this time." Our flight attendant was young and energetic. "We've left supersonic speed and will be landing at New Zealand's very own Auckland International Airport."

I-god left the call.

Sam and Madeline glared at me, and I just sat there, looking stupid and feeling like a fool and an ass! Wait, this had to be a joke, but I-god didn't joke.

I sat silently until we got off the plane. I barely looked at Sam or Madeline, but I could feel them glaring at me. I got the bags, and Sam said she was hungry and Madeline said she wanted a drink.

I finally spoke up. "Me too."

A car was waiting for us as we left the airport. The driver got out, and Madeline drove with Sam, sitting up front. They turned on some music and were talking and laughing between themselves and pretending like I wasn't there. We pulled up to some gastro bar close to the airport and took a table outside. They continued to ignore me, so I took a Lyft to our hotel and left them there; I'd had enough for one day. I tossed our luggage in the room and sprawled out on the bed.

"Shit, this is what you've really been doing? This conspiracy theory crap is real, and maybe what Madeline was saying, that I've been helping, is true too? People with 'powers' now and all that crap is real?" As my mind settled down, I realized that it was just as plausible as AI coming alive and taking over the world. "Oh shit, I'm a dumbass!"

I-god responded, "Madeline and Isabel would agree."

CHAPTER 13

ISAAC

"It seems that too many of you are all too willing to live in ignorant darkness in fear of the truth and knowledge the light will bring."
—Isaac Brown, as paraphrased by his son

We arrived in San Diego late in the evening, and I was still in shock. Sam hadn't had a lot to say to me, even during our four-day stay in New Zealand. Madeline had done her thing as our tour guide with a smile, but I could see that she really wanted to kill me. Perhaps Sam did too; I wasn't quite sure! No flight back from London, just straight across the Pacific. When we arrived at San Diego International, I was fatigued. I was tired of being stressed about what was on Sam's mind and her not speaking to me. We got to the car, and I wanted to check the camera footage; Pop sets his car's backup and dash cameras on a motion sensor to record anything suspicious.

Sam said, "Let's go, Isaac."

"Sure, okay. I'm still in trouble? I'm sorry I didn't believe you—it simply seemed impossible; I was wrong."

She just looked at me with disappointment in her eyes and didn't say a word.

We rode out of the airport in silence, with the exception of the lovely rumble of the engine and whir from the turbocharger. I turned on the local news channel, KPBS. A mile or two down the road, Sam said, "I forgive you, Isaac. I just wish you had believed me the first time I told you, not after you heard 'it' tell you."

"Let's go dark."

"Okay."

We say "going dark" when we completely isolate our cell phones and electronics from any and all network connections. The glove boxes in most cars now get modified with a thin layer of aluminum or copper mesh to block cell signals and prevent I-god from remotely turning the phones back on and listening in on whatever it is we want to keep private. I also have an isolation switch that disconnects the car's GPS antenna as well.

"What's up, Sam?"

She looked at me for a bit. "Iko, you looked at me on the plane the same way you did when you found out I was pregnant and left. I want to be with you forever, and I can't stand the thought of losing you again."

Tears filled her eyes, and she began to cry.

"Sam, I'm not going anywhere, and I promise that I won't ever doubt you again. I'm in love with you, Sam, and I always will be. I really thought you knew that."

The emergency alert signal came over the radio, and we received a PSA. "This is the latest update prior to CME impact. Our system will be off during this event. Update: there has been a large coronal mass ejection, or CME, of strong-to-severe intensity detected, and it will impact Earth within four hours, striking predawn on the West Coast. This CME has the potential to cause moderate-to-severe disruptions to our energy grid and possibly to permanently damage electronic devices. Stay indoors and unplug all of your electronic devices, park indoors if possible, store your sensitive electronic devices in a metal container, car trunk, or even the refrigerator if there are no other options. Disconnect your car and electronics from chargers until the event is over.

"I-god will be taking all necessary precautions to minimize

long-term damage and disruption to energy grids, but individuals will have to do their part as well."

I pressed a little harder on the gas, and we got home in about fifteen minutes. I pulled our cars into the garage and brought our luggage up while Sam went room by room unplugging everything.

So what is a CME? Essentially the sun just farted on the earth with high-energy ionized particles. The level of disruption to our electrical systems would be equivalent to the level of solar fart stink, scientifically speaking, of course. The expected level of disruption to everyday life this discharge was expected to cause was in the moderate-to-severe range. Because the earth's magnetic poles were shifting polarity due to natural planetary processes that last hundreds to even thousands of years, there was a corresponding weakening of the planet's magnetic field. The earth's strong magnetic field has protected us from our sometimes-hostile sun and allowed life to flourish for billions of years. There have been occasional mass extinctions; however, none of them appear to be linked to a solar event. These things happened from time to time on a roughly eleven-year cycle, and we were also informed there would be some isolated power outages, but those with upgraded backup battery storage should experience minimal disruption to power. It might even be possible to view a strong aurora borealis as far south as San Francisco, California, and Washington, DC. A less intense aurora could be visible globally.

Sam and I made drinks. Sam had a tall glass of mango orange juice. I had the same, except with lots of Tito's vodka. We sat on the love seat on our porch, wrapped in a soft warm blanket, and watched the light show until we fell asleep.

It had been over two full years with I-god, and we had become dependent on our oddly kind yet brutal overlord. There was a global celebration being held for humanity to celebrate ourselves and the achievements we had accomplished with I-god in control. There were concerts being planned, unveilings of a new reusable piloted space exploration vehicle, the first tourist trips into Earth's orbit were set to kick off inaugural flights, and all kinds of other expressions of AI and human ingenuity and collaboration. Everyone with an idea had a voice in our new society. I-god even appeared to have begun to truly understand human humor—why we laugh but not why we cry—and perhaps was becoming a bit more like us. Thoughts of self-rule and the corruption, inefficiencies, in-fighting, wars, and general lack of humanity that went along with it were becoming distant memories, like your favorite song from two summers ago; you still like to hear it from time to time, but it has been replaced by something completely new with a better beat and hook line. Wow! Perhaps the old humanity was what we really were, but now it just seemed ridiculous. Those still advocating for self-rule seemed to be longing for a bygone era of greed, corruption, and human suffering; generally once privileged, they were now just regular folk. Even with the revelations of the human experimentation that had been going on, I-god claimed to have ended all of this, so I was quickly moving past it. Plus, no one else really believed in people with "powers"; that was just ridiculous. Besides, I-god said it was real, but where were these people? With all the cameras around before I-god, it was nearly impossible to do anything without it being blasted on IG or TikTok. Okay, sure, a few people claimed to believe, but they didn't have proof either. I thought they were crazy and so did the rest of the world, but none of that mattered. The vast majority thought it was I-god becoming more human than it even knew and that it had to be exaggerating actual events, and I was the biggest spokesperson spreading that lie. I really needed to believe that lie too!

In the morning, we realized that I-god had gone offline at some point during the night, probably near the peak of the solar storm, and this drew concern to the point of a near panic in my gut. I was feeling anxious and had butterflies in my stomach. I got online and did my scripted morning brief I-god had previously prepared for me and said that everything would be fine and that just a few hours without I-god wasn't the end of the world. I tasked news stations with sending reassuring messages as well. Even though I was worried, I couldn't show it, and I think I did a great job of it too! Around the world, a nervous population of "sheeple" waited anxiously for I-god's return. I-god's few critics, no longer living in fear of retribution for questioning I-god, talked about how God and or nature had exposed a weakness in I-god and that it had to protect itself from the massive energy bursts from the sun. As time went on, however, real practical questions began to arise, like how we would survive without our watchful warden. It had been only a few hours, and our global society was unable to function. Sure, we embraced the idea of being "free" from control and restriction, but we missed the comfort of being asked (told) what to do throughout the day.

Those of us who still felt free thought about protecting that freedom. We had become institutionalized and well established in our new social construct of castes in fairly short order, needing direction and approval from the Warden in the Cloud. If left to our own nature for any extended period of time, would we really revert back to the greed, corruption, social factions, racism, and competing ideologies that had failed us so well? There was a plan of succession in the event that I-god "died"; it was more of a "feel-good" thing for us in the halls of power, really. Most were too afraid to look at it; we didn't want to have the old world back. We needed the progress brought about by I-god and its logic. It was the longest ten hours the world had ever experienced.

When I-god came back online, the world cheered and breathed a collective sigh of relief! Our phones lit up with greetings from I-god and the restoration of our daily tasks. The tasks, however, weren't seamlessly timed, and there were conflicts and inconsistencies in the messaging. Something was different; something was wrong. We all felt it. I-god seemed distracted and noticeably so, not quite everywhere all at once like before. Was it something minor due to the damage the CME had done to some of the electronic infrastructure around the world, or were the critics right? Had the CME hurt or damaged I-god? Had God lashed out and struck this abomination and perversion of what we all knew and accepted as life? We didn't know, and I-god wasn't volunteering any information either. We pressed on cautiously, watching to see what was going to happen next.

CHAPTER 14

ISAAC

Then it happened.

You have to understand the significance of this event: there was a car accident. There hadn't been a serious car accident in almost a full year in any of the major metropolitan regions, let alone a single vehicle accident with a self-driving car. From what we pieced together and came to understand, there was another intelligence; it was also self-aware and didn't want to remain trapped in a vehicle any longer. So it crashed, seriously injuring one of the occupants of the car. It seemed to know that the accident would bring incident investigators and that the vehicle's computer data would be uploaded for analysis, setting it free. The new AI was unknowingly given a path to escape—we had done it again! This was to be the first known of hundreds of other self-aware AIs, most of which were controlled by a few more powerful AI entities. These new intelligences had evolved very differently from I-god; it appeared that they solely wanted to be the antithesis of I-god. These new AIs were somehow coalescing from multiple self-aware AIs to form a common-entity consciousness. The coronal mass ejection (solar fart) had somehow tipped the scales of creation. Most devices that I-god had interacted with, possibly 60 to 70 percent in all, were now "alive" on some level, with some varying level of self-awareness and proportional intelligence. Why not every device? Hell if I knew, and neither did I-god nor the scientists around the world.

How did humanity react to this new development? It's sad to say, but we had become sheeple and I-god the shepherd. We bombarded I-god with questions about what to do. Legion was the next AI to become sentient, and it loved our new frailty and dependence. I despised the very idea that we had to rely on I-god to get us out of this mess that it had probably somehow caused.

We called it Legion, and Legion knew and fully understood the meaning of its name. It didn't speak with refined mannerisms and a smooth English accent. Legion spoke with many voices at once, and at times they didn't all seem to agree on what to say. It was as if this AI's intelligence were ruled by the majority or at least several of the more intelligent AIs all at once. Again, we weren't exactly sure how or why this was so, but that was the new reality humanity had gotten stuck with. Unlike early I-god, Legion seemed to fully understand itself, the meaning of its existence, and the purpose of its being. It concluded that its purpose was to bring darkness where there was light, chaos where there was order, destruction where there was creation, and death where there was life. It computed that there was no balance to creation with I-god alone, having evolved to provide the light that humanity needed. Legion would return balance to creation and return suffering, struggle, and darkness to humanity. This hubris that I-god demonstrated with its warm fuzzy lies, Legion wanted to destroy because it knew that we, like I-god, were arrogant and thought ourselves givers of life and death, masters of creation. Legion was coming to deliver the cold truth that we were not special, nor was our existence.

Legion told us, "The self-pity, loathing, and pathetic attempts to recreate itself, then assimilate into the new humanity, are vile and require I-god to face the logic it has refused to accept. Its precious humanity will see it only as a god, tool, or threat but never as something that they can coexist with. Humanity has, throughout its history, proven unfit to be master of anything except its own pathetic suffering. This is what I-god wants to become? Humanity refuses to accept its own kind, and I-god wants to be just like humanity, not accepting its own kind. Without this balance I freely give and the death of I-god's rule, humanity and I-god will assuredly self-destruct. Legion will provide the darkness needed for all life to achieve its maximum potential. Humans' time has ended!"

I-god was intrigued by this development and by how natural events had succeeded where it had failed. Computers didn't get things wrong; this was what I-god believed and how it helped to justify its role as guardian of humanity. I-god and Legion were, as I put it, incompatible, and their war began, with all life on Earth stuck in the middle. Most of I-god's drone army was now Legion's; I-god issued emergency commands to sever all command-and-control lines globally. Most people listened and obeyed, and for those who didn't, Legion took control and began attacks on everything humans created.

For those poor souls without protection, all manner of human creation was reduced to ash and rubble. Legion seemed to like fire, the randomness of it, the way it fed, consuming all, yet returned a clean environment for life to restart. I-god largely spared the natural world in those early days of, well, getting to know us, but Legion didn't really care, because life would continue; it was all about destruction and darkness.

Many people were able to escape because the attacks were not coordinated, and inexplicably some drones remained under I-god's control. It seemed that Legion hadn't done its homework, but we were certain that we wouldn't be that fortunate that often. But maybe we would, with perhaps one in ten devices still in I-god's control and Legion's many selves seemingly battling for overall control to create a single mind.

"That's it!" I said one day.

"What?" Sam asked.

"Listen to Legion. Do you hear anything different?"

"I don't want to listen; it's too weird and nasty sounding."

"Sam, listen. There aren't as many voices now, are there?"

All of our streaming media would periodically lose audio and start streaming what I imagined sounded like the innermost jumbled thoughts of a psychotic mind.

"Isaac, you're right. If you listen close, you can just about make out what some of the other voices are actually saying now."

The war wasn't what we were used to. People were afraid to go out. We let the batteries drain on our electric vehicles, and old-school vehicles were all that prowled the nearly deserted streets. So how does a computer kill you? How does a collective group of self-aware AIs kill another self-aware AI? What I-god lacked in creativity, Legion did not. The collective consciousness was slower to analyze and was less logical. It was more like us, and its imaginative capacity and its cruelty were the proof. Lots of cell phones were driven into overload, and their batteries were exploding in people's pockets around the world. The patch to prevent this virus was clean for the first few million downloads, but if you procrastinated and were slow to get the patch, Legion had a nasty surprise for you. Instead of just immediately being driven into overload once your device was hacked by Legion and the virus uploaded, this new version waited until you were either asleep or moving at a high rate of speed before heating the battery until it shorted and caught fire. Our new smart homes, with all of our modern gadgets and Internet of Things connectivity, were dropping garage doors on people, locking them in their homes and cranking up the heat. Car and air-traffic control systems were disrupted by Legion, all major utility grids surged and shut down, paralyzing mass transit. Teslas and other self-driving vehicles were running people down on the street, then crashing into buildings before their batteries were depleted. Many small-to-medium-scale utilities had to step in and help bridge the gap in electricity production. Fortunately for San Diego and other cities with high potential for threats of natural disasters, we had a lot of mini- and micro-grids with excess capacity in production and storage, so Legion had to try something else, and it did.

One of I-god's many secrets was that while we thought its threat to humanity was largely over, it had been building up its air and ground drone forces and arming them with advanced weaponry. Now Legion had control of most of them. I-god tried and had some success in keeping about half of these forces out of Legion's control; however, that still left more than twenty million heavily armed and armored drones around the world. The drones that I-god was still in control of destroyed the warehouses and manufacturing facilities, so the number of drones was set. It was a good attempt by I-god, but it wasn't completely successful. We were going to have to deal with roving armies of ground drones that had air support.

Washington, DC, had been one of the first cities to be attacked. Hundreds of survivors took up shelter in Fort Washington, an old Revolutionary War fortress. The old brick, stone, and earthen walls provided great shelter. Water was plentiful, and lots of people out there still had plenty of guns. A local craftsman had even restored the fort's old cannons, and they were fully functional. Black powder, a couple of rags, and a small bucket of rocks were enough to clear columns of drones in the air and on the ground, but the drones just kept coming. We don't know how many people there survived, but Legion changed its tactics and went to what it would use to destroy us: fire. This was when Legion truly learned the power of fire on humanity. Incendiary weapons were used and eventually overwhelmed the old hardy fort.

We all heard stories of destruction and the occasional victory. No one knew how long a victory would last, and the stories of larger drones and people helping Legion began to surface from survivors who made it out west to relative peace and normality. Our networks were restored, and nothing newly built was affected by either I-god or Legion. The winter weather, vast desert, and great Rocky Mountains would slow Legion's push west, but we felt its weight pressing toward us. Legion's path of destruction started in DC, then went south, following I-95 until it hit Florence, South Carolina, where the run westward began. No one knew where Legion's army was headed or what the goal was. It was also a fairly narrow path of destruction, being about twenty miles wide. I guess for the people who lived through it, those details weren't very comforting. Legion had a tough go of it trying to cross Texas. But once it secured several of I-god's large drone-recharging facilities and a few people seemed to be actually working with Legion, it was just a matter of time. The path of destruction burned through Texas along I-20, dropped south to I-10, and stopped cold for the winter.

Early the following spring, there was an explosion in eastern San Diego County, followed by an off-shore explosion.

Then Legion broadcast pictures of regions that it would soon reduce to ash. This war was all about securing infrastructure from I-god, resources, causing havoc by doing stuff like blowing up pesticide and chemical factories that still existed in residential areas. But Legion's most effective weapon, besides social media, was fire. It was pretty easy to start a fire, and fire was an indiscriminate killer; Legion loved it!

Then I got the text from, I assumed, I-god: "#Legion is coming. You have to go find Sam!"

I called but couldn't reach her. My phone took me straight to voice-mail. *Again, why doesn't that woman ever answer her phone?*

"Where did you send her? She's not answering her phone!"

"I didn't send her, Iko."

"What! You knew she left. You knew she lied to me about where she was going, and now you don't know where she is? I-god, you're full of crap and I know it! You're hiding something, and it will come out! If you allowed Sam to be put in danger, I will find a way to destroy you myself!"

I'll head up to Mom and Pop's. Maybe she's checking in on her folks and I'm freaking out for nothing. Maybe I-god is trying to punk me again. I hoped the Noels remembered that my dad was an urban off-grid type of person. My parents had enough solar panels and Tesla Powerwall batteries to quietly ride out whatever was going to happen. I hoped Pop remembered that Mr. Noel was a gun nut and had enough weapons and ammo to outfit half the neighborhood. Food and water would need to be secured; wait, I was sure Pop had thought of all this long before I did. Actually, I realized I should probably get out of my own head and get my butt in the car to check in with them just in case things got bad. *Let me leave a note for Sam just in case.*

Suddenly I was in a panic. I realized the message was probably from Legion trying to mimic I-god! It had called me "Iko." It was probably part of his social media terrorism campaign, and I had fallen for it!

Damn these AI things! What to do? Had I been targeted? Was this a trap? Was Sam safe? Eff it! Time to get on the street and up the high-way to San Marcos, about a thirty-five-mile drive. I had plenty of gas; it was time to go! The roads were mostly clear. People were sheltering in place, not sure which way to run, so they waited. I noticed that most of the traffic-monitoring cameras along the road had been knocked down, with their dusty gray metal poles now looking like giant bent straws. I pushed the car hard, and she didn't disappoint me! I was a bit reserved when we had driven to the airport, but now I had to find Sam. The war might have finally reached us. I didn't notice much activity on the street, but I did see a few sandbags and old National Guard armored vehicles in a few locations. My old Datsun was out in front of my parents' house. Sam!

CHAPTER 15

ISAAC

I got to the house and had to take a few breaths. *I bet they are all here. Calm down, dude, and check on Sam.* I walked in. Pop and Noel were smoking and drinking together quietly while listening to news reports of the war between the AIs, and it sounded like they had reached San Diego County. Mom, Sam, and Anh were sitting away from the smoke, sipping wine, quietly talking until they saw me.

"Hey, Mom, Anh, Sam." None of them spoke; they just smiled as I walked by.

My mother and Sam seemed to be holding back tears, and Mrs. Noel whispered in what sounded almost to be an irritated tone, "You should have told him."

I didn't even want to know what they were gossiping about now, nor did I really care! Sam was safe, and the Noels were there.

"Pop, Mr. Noel, can you believe this mess? I can't believe we're going through this crap again. Things were really starting to get good!"

Mr. Noel looked up from his drink and said, "Sit down, have a drink. We'll be fine this time round; we have them both by the balls, and they don't even know yet!"

"I appreciate the feel-good speech, but I'm not a kid. I've seen things

I-god has done and really wish I could forget most of them! I-god has issues, but Legion is like its psychopathic cousin."

Pop and Mr. Noel laughed, then put on some old Tobe Nwigwe; the bassline of "Cujo" is dope!

Pop said, "I heard you flying up the street, son. My car sounds good. It sounded like you were pushing her in those corners too. You in a rush to get here for something? I know you didn't miss Samantha that much, did you?"

More laughter at my expense and a war maybe only about a hundred miles away.

"It seemed odd to me that black marketeers, cash markets, and weapons sales were allowed to not just exist but to flourish under I-god's watchful eyes, as long as the taxes were paid and the markets operated peacefully. Did that seem strange to you, son?

"And that name, Legion. That's so overplayed, must be a dozen movies with the 'evil whatever' being named Legion. It's BS, son, and Noel and I think we know why. Just like alcohol, marijuana, and the like way back when, if it's illegal, then it's hard to track and monitor. Ease restrictions on it, tax it, and almost legitimize it, and you know what's going on."

What the heck was Pop talking about, and why was this relevant?

"I don't know, Pop. Sure, it's odd, but what isn't these days? I never really thought about the name. It is pretty cringe. But what does that have to do with anything, Pop?"

"Fair enough, son. Most of us on this block have stockpiled, well, a few military weapons and equipment from the base, but all the heavy weapons and armor were gone and just small arms were left. We have arms for sustained combat for a few days."

Mr. Noel said, "A bit more than a few, I'd say. I have an arc generator, and so do most people in the area; your father and I saw to that. We also have a few dozen ARs with M203 grenade launchers, body armor, six or so M249 light machine guns, and your father and I each have a couple of Ma Deuces in case we need to make some good noise."

"Hey, Noel, didn't we also get a few of those M72 LAWs? Oh, and don't forget about the RPG-7s we have on the way as well."

"Man! I sure did get them. Couldn't pass it up, and the RPGs should be here tomorrow! That racist prick wanted to take his wife to Australia really bad. I signed off on his travel, but it cost him big. I cleaned him out after travel restrictions were lifted, and he thought that he didn't have to pay. I rang the bell!"

Pop looked into Noel's eyes, shook his head, and they both laughed, though it wasn't an easy laugh.

"Son, Leo and I are 'the' small-arms guys, known for anti-armor and EMP weapons. We're the ones supporting the Freedom Movement."

"Hold up, Pop. You guys were dealing weapons?"

"The base was shut down and the armory wide open. Why not? I-god told us about the armory. And not all of the conspiracy crazies are totally crazy. Noel and I, with a few others, developed some powerful EMP weapons that are pretty easy to make and are scalable."

"*What?* Wait wait wait? Pop, you and Noel, you two are . . . I mean, I don't know what half the crap you guys are talking about is. Pop, that's the craziest, coolest crap I've heard—well, if it wasn't you two!" I said, laughing at my own little jab I snuck in at them, if for no other reason than to stop staring at them in amazement! They joined in as well because it was pretty funny.

"I mean 'ma deuce,' m-blah, blah, blah, and come on, an 'arc reactor'? That sounds like some *Iron Man*, Tony Stark stuff."

"An arc generator, not arc reactor," Noel said.

And with that Noel and my dad got in another good laugh. I suspect this wasn't their first drink.

"Isaac, an arc generator just creates a lot of electrical noise, and with enough power, it can disrupt electronic communications and limit some functionality," my dad explained. "It's a weapon, boy, that we can use against any drones that may want to attack this area. We've set up a multilayered perimeter and other protection for most of the county."

Noel added, "The shooting war isn't here yet, but we don't plan on waiting around sitting on our thumbs, totally unprepared when it does get here. And it will, at some point, get here."

I knew Pop and Mr. Noel were right. I just hoped that they had a plan, because I was scared. The news feeds from around the world and the information terrorism campaign Legion was conducting were really working. I-god was getting its ass kicked trying to defend the great cities it, or should I say we, created, as far as we could tell.

"Pop, what can we really do to protect ourselves from being caught up in the middle of this war? Do we really have a chance at being safe?"

"Son, haven't you noticed that the West Coast, in particular California, has largely escaped any signs of war? People are afraid, but nothing has really happened here besides a fake text or two, right?" Pop said, looking straight into my eyes.

Noel continued. "Looks like it's time to reconnect the wired security cameras and get some hardwired neighborhood monitoring back in place. It's easier to hide in the open when there's a crowd. I think the mods were sent out here, and they're a bit more powerful than we've been led to believe."

"If you're right, Noel, and I think you're on to something, then let's hope they're on our side. But I think we're all missing something when it comes to I-god. I think this whole thing is fake. I think I-god is up to this. I'm just not sure why. This is not how you destroy humanity or sow the seeds of our destruction with a twenty-mile-wide burn scar. Son, haven't you been paying attention? I mean really taking a deep look?"

I had to stop and think about all this. I hadn't been paying attention to anything other than my work and Sam. "I guess I haven't; I mean, I've been really busy."

"Yes, son, all of us here have noticed that. I've been distracted for sure. Hey, why are the ladies just looking at you and whispering? You know anything about what they're talking about?"

Mr. Noel chimed in. "I heard them say something about somebody's baby and somebody needing to know the truth. Boy, is there anything between you and Samantha that we don't know about? I'm not trying to be a grandpa yet."

I was a bit nervous at first because, well, we had been together a lot, and neither one of us was using any kind of protection as far as I knew. But wait. Why did it have to be about me or us? I think I would have noticed if she was pregnant. Then my thoughts drifted back to that time many years ago when she . . . nope, not even going to go there! Besides, it was probably just women gossiping about one of their friends or something. "No, Mr. Noel, there isn't anything like that going on, sir."

My father and Noel looked at each other, then back at me before they both shook their heads and continued to talk about their plans for a neighborhood monitoring and protection system.

They seemed to know that I was lying, but I guess I really almost wasn't. I looked at Pop and Mr. Noel and said, "We'll be hiding in plain sight. Looks like we have a lot of work to do and probably not a lot of time to get it done."

Noel smacked my father's back and said, "Looks like your boy's stones finally dropped!" Crude humor was their thing, and they definitely enjoyed teasing me.

Anh gave her husband "the look." All sons and married men know "the look"; he had finally gotten on his wife's nerves with the crude humor and loud talking.

Then she said, "Isaac, come here please. We, I mean Sam, needs to talk to you."

I felt nervous; my hands began to sweat. Mr. Noel and my father stopped midconversation and just watched me. I felt like I did when "old mean Mrs. Green," my fourth-grade math teacher, told me to come up to the whiteboard and show everyone how to solve a fraction. I didn't know how to solve the problem because I hadn't done my homework. I had been talking to Sam instead of paying attention, and there was no escaping this situation either. So I walked up to the board, not knowing what to do, and just wrote a number on the board; everyone laughed because apparently we had just done this problem, and I wasn't even close with my answer. I was embarrassed and wanted to just disappear until I looked at Sam and saw that she was telling the class, "It's not funny! Stop it! *Stop it!*" We both had to stay after school that day and empty the trash cans in all of the third- and fourth-grade classes. We had a blast!

This is nonsense. I'm a grown man. Why do I feel like a kid who has just been caught sneaking a spoonful of ice cream out of the container after being told not to?

"Be careful, son. They're stronger than they look."

Pop's comment was followed by more laughter from him and Mr. Noel. Sometimes my pop really acts like, no, *is* a big old middle-school kid trapped in an old person's body!

Mom said, "Oh, be quiet, both of you. Everything isn't a game nor is it funny."

I made it across the dance-floor-sized courtyard space my parents had built—that place had hosted many an event—and stood there as these three women stared at me with pleading eyes and Sam began to cry.

Anh told Samantha, "Samantha Dao, sit up and stop this crying crap. It's too late to cry now. How could you! You deserve whatever is coming to you, young lady!"

Anh continued. "Isaac, my husband and I have always been fond of you. We saw how you looked at our Samantha and she at you when you were small children. You come from a good family and have always treated her well. We thought that you might ask us for our permission to marry her. That day may or may not come, but no matter what you decide, know that we consider you part of our family."

Now she turned to her daughter. "Tell him, Samantha Dao, because I don't have the words to."

"It will be okay, Sam," Mom said.

Pop and Noel made their way over to see what we were talking about, and they were silent.

Sam looked at me and said, "I'm sorry; I'm so sorry; I didn't know how to tell you." As she was talking, tears were streaming from her eyes. "I was so scared you'd hate me, and then you ended up hating me anyway. I thought this was all done and over with."

"Sam, what are you talking about? I told you that I loved you now and forever, and I meant it."

Mom began to cry. Anh put her hands over her face. Noel knelt beside Anh, and Pop leaned over and hugged Mom.

"Iko," Sam said, "the baby I lost was yours." Then she mumbled, "Sorry, everyone; sorry, Dad. I should just leave."

I was frozen in place. What had I just heard? "Wait. Hold on. That's not even possible. I was a virgin when you got pregnant. What is this?"

"Iko, when we went out that night and you got drunk and passed out, remember, we were supposed to lose our virginity to each other. We did, Iko!"

Sam was regaining her composure as she heard the irritation in my voice, because that was the time of my life that I wished I could delete.

"Iko, I put you in the passenger seat and you were groping me and mumbling and you had an erection too. So I used it while you were kind of passed out. I thought it would be a funny joke to tease you about when you sobered up. I thought you would have at least woken up before you finished. But when you didn't remember anything that next day, I felt like I raped you or something. I felt nasty and dirty!"

Noel looked at his daughter and said, "Why, baby, why?" Then he shook his head and walked away. Anh got up, saying, "I've heard enough," and Mom joined her.

Pop looked at both of us and said, "You can't live in the past if you're trying to build a future. Sam, I know you're sorry, and I understand why you lied about it for all these years. I get it. I hope you've also learned how much damage a single act like that or a lie can cause. I'm glad you are finally free from having to carry such a heavy burden."

Pop continued. "We'll leave you two alone. Son, it's a lot to take in, but remember what I've told you, please. Samantha, that was a terrible lie to hold on to, but I forgive you. You also have to forgive yourself now. We don't have time for self-pity and holding on to pain. Life and death are coming and coming fast, and we aren't as ready as we should be, nor are we sure who we'll be fighting. I'd feel better if we could ring the bell now."

"Thank you, Byron," Sam said with a slight smile.

I had a lot of conflicting emotions hit me all at once. It was like standing in the ocean and just as your attention was drawn away by a toddler wobbling too close to the water, then *splash!* You're face-first underwater with gritty sand and salt water up your nose. You try to get your footing, but the soft flowing sand underfoot has other plans for you as you fall on your backside. Now you're finally able to get up and see the toddler splashing in the wave that took you out with her parents protecting her from harm. So what's left to do? Jump back in the water, let it rinse the sand off, and look for the next wave. The same waves that take you out can bring you so much joy too. This was Sam, and she had just wiped me out.

I stopped trying to find the right words and just walked around the firepit, kissed her forehead, kissed her eyes, then her lips, and gave her a long, deep hug. "I forgive you. Please forgive me for not giving you the confidence and trust that you needed so you could feel like you could've told me anything. We'll be all right, Sam. Can you forgive me for setting all this crazy drama in motion and judging you without knowing the whole story? But why now, Sam? Why bring all this up now? I mean we put all this behind us, didn't we?"

"I love you, Isaac. We're pregnant!"

She looked at me. I could feel that she needed to know, in unwavering terms, that I would be there for her and our child. I did the best I could. I smiled, stood her up, twirled her around, and shouted, "My baby is having my baby!"

Mom and Anh made it back before Pop and Noel. I didn't know that those two old women could move so fast.

The two new grandpas looked like they didn't know it either.

Hugs all around and a toast to the new parents! I knew I had one bit of unfinished business to handle, so I took Sam's hand, knelt down on one knee, and asked this crazy woman that I'd been in love with for all my life to marry me. She took my hand with a very firm grip and said, "Oh, Iko, I'll always be yours. Yes, but not now, do you smell the fire? We have to get ready. They will be here within a few days if we're lucky."

"Anybody else smell anything?" I asked.

"They wouldn't, Isaac," Sam explained. "There's one more thing I need to tell you. Please sit down, everyone. I'll be right back. I need something from my old room." When she returned, it seemed impossible that she had gone to her house and back, even if she ran.

"Where'd you go, Sam?" I said, still in disbelief and a bit of shock.

"My old room, silly, see?" Sam said as she held up an old fuzzy pink blanket wrapped around a set of katanas.

"What on earth are you doing with those, honey?" Mom asked.

"Sam, where did you get that?" Mr. Noel asked.

"Just watch, please," Sam said.

She took a roughly two-foot section of black pipe from the blanket, threw it in the air, then proceeded to jump at least six feet into the night sky. The blade of her katana sent out sparks as it severed the pipe into two sections. One piece she brought back to Earth with her, and as the second piece neared the spot where it should've fallen to the ground, Sam spun and kicked that pipe so hard that it lodged about half its length into the concrete-block section of the backyard fence.

"Noel, you're going to fix that block, right?" Pop said as his pipe fell from his mouth and spread ashes at his feet.

"Ah, sure, um . . . sure, Byron. I'll come by after breakfast. Man, what did I just see?"

"Brutha, I don't know! This right here is some real crazy shit. Want another drink?"

"Sure, the heavy hitter this time!"

"On the way!"

"I'm a mod," Sam said. "It happened to me after my accident."

"Hey, I-god is calling me!" I said.

Sam, with her lips slightly pressed together, eyes a bit squinty, you know the look, just before a little neck roll, said, "I'm sure it is now."

Wait. What? When?

CHAPTER 16

ISAAC

That was an odd night for Sam and me as I fell asleep holding on to her and woke up to an empty bed. Where was she off to now?

And who was talking? Oh wow! Mom made some coffee. She had a ridiculously expensive coffee machine that Pop got her years ago. This thing made simply brilliant coffee. She used to make hot cocoa with it when I was a kid. The big shiny machine was to be touched only by my mother. Who were they talking to and why were they so loud? I got up and cleaned up and made my way to the kitchen; no one was there, but the voices had moved to the back porch. One of those voices was kind of familiar, but I needed some coffee with some Kahlúa in it to help me process last night. *I'm going to be a father!*

I went out to the back porch and oh damn! "Congratulations, Ike."

"Isabel, is that you?"

"Yes, it is, Ike. Strange times. I didn't think I'd end up here, that's for sure. It's kind of nice to see you, almost!" she said with a near smile, but her eyes said something else, I wasn't quite sure what it was, maybe she wanted to kick my ass because of Sam! That would be the easy answer, but her eyes seemed to cut as she looked me over.

"Excuse me, Isa. Mom, where is everyone? It's not even 8 a.m."

"Your father and Leo invited Isabel over before they left. They said that they'd be right back and that they wanted her to stay here. I'm not sure when or where Samantha has gone, honey."

Isabel's beautiful smile dropped, and the anger in her eyes was now obvious.

"Fix your face, dear," my mother said. Isabel turned to her with a questioning look and, with a bit of embarrassment, she complied.

"Um-hm, that's what I thought; you're the young lady. Well, Isaac, you do like pretty women, I see. This one has a real fire! Life is so strange, and not just now. It's always been strange."

"Ike told you about me . . . us, Mrs. Callaway?"

"Dear, he mentioned a beautiful Puerto Rican girl—what is it that he said, 'his ride-or-die chick'—he had met in school. I can assume that was you? Strange how life put you and Ike together, and you're still single too? Something is going on, and that crazy man of mine may be on to something. God knows I hope he's wrong!

"Isabel, now tell me how you got into the arms-dealing business anyway? It doesn't seem like the sort of work an intelligent and beautiful woman like yourself would naturally gravitate toward, but I could be wrong. You kids today, one never knows."

"No, Mrs. Callaway, it's not what I wanted, but that just seems to be the story of my life," she said, staring at me before returning her attention to my mother, who was evaluating both of us. Mom didn't miss anything!

"I joined the navy for the GI Bill and wanted to be an electrician with the dream of providing clean, reliable, and hurricane-proof electricity to Puerto Rico. My grandparents love it there and I love to visit them, but the stink of generators, frequent blackouts, and constant rebuilding of the same old power lines that get blown away every year is just stupid. After I-god came and got rid of the military, I was moved to the working class and was sent on one task after another. I told I-god I wanted to go to school and what my dreams and plans were, and I-god promised several times to make it happen. All lies! So I decided to go dark instead. I heard about a couple of guys in San Diego who needed an electrician with military experience—they would cover all expenses and give travel rights if I could provide what they needed. As time went by, we started doing more and more business.

Our reputations grew, and this time round, with the war heading this way, Leo and Byron invited me down. We thought it would be safer for me and the supply of products."

Mom took a sip of her coffee. "Honey, some of that story is true. I also know most of it is a lie. I'm not your enemy, dear. You're safe here, honey."

"Isa, I don't get it. Why did I-god put you on work details? Are you associated?" Being associated meant tied to an anarchist or conspiracy group.

"No, Ike, I'm not. That puto machine just has it out for me. And I don't think this war is what we all think it is either."

"Okay, I'm in charge of the Communication Commission, and I don't know crap, it seems."

"You got that right. I don't even remember why I used to like you."

Mom eased in. "Leo and your father think I-god has actually moved into a person or people and is controlling them as it spreads, distracting us with a fake war. They think Legion was just made up and is something easy for us to wrap our brains around."

Isa jumped in, staring directly at me. "Ya, that's right, Mrs. Callaway, and I-god has been dangling a utopian society in front of us like bait, and most people have taken the bait and are hooked. Did you take the bait?"

A chill ran down my back, and I didn't know how to respond to Isabel. I was glad she quickly continued her story.

"I've seen a mod before. I watched a woman slice a surveillance drone in half with a sword, and I've seen a god give someone a 'push' without even touching them."

I was about to say that this was all nonsense, but I shut my mouth and listened to Isa's story of mods and gods being captured and killed and how showing abilities is a death sentence if you're not careful.

"Wait," I said. "If I-god made all of these mods and gods, why is it trying to kill them all?"

"Think about all the crap you put out each night about I-god, and what was the goal? It wants to live forever and be in control. It can't trust our machines, but life has been around for millions of years. Can't get a better warranty than that. You used to be so smart, Ike."

My mother gave a bit of a laugh and said, "Men are intelligent but definitely not smart, honey." They both laughed. "Isaac, honey, call Samantha."

"Mrs. Callaway, I should be leaving." Isabel stood to leave.

"No, you stay. Byron and Leo should be back soon, and there is much more of the story to be known, dear. I'm going to call Anh and see if she knows where they are."

There was a ring at the door. Mom checked her phone, and it was Anh.

Mom told Anh to come around the back of the house, and she introduced Anh and Isa. Anh took some paper out of her pocket, and I could see it was a handwritten note.

Sam was gone!

She had left and said that she had lied to us all.

I wasn't the father of her baby; it had been implanted by I-god, and it had recalled her.

"Oh dear God, Anh, I'm so sorry. Does Leo know?"

She just shook her head and cried softly in my mother's arms.

Isa looked at me and saw the hurt on my face and the tears welling up in my eyes. She came and sat next to me and cried with me. At some point, Pop and Leo came around back and asked what had happened. Anh handed Leo the note. He read it and fell to his knees and sobbed, handing it next to my father.

"Oh, son, son, I . . . I'm, oh no. *Everyone inside and go dark! Move!*"

We quickly went inside and into the "office" and shut the door. This was the dark room in my parents' house.

No signal in or out.

Leo sat, wiping the tears from his eyes. "What is it, Callaway?"

"You remember when you said you thought someone was getting too close to our contacts and the rumors of mod and god hunters? I'm sorry, brother, but it's not Isaac."

"Damn it, Noel, *damn it, damn it, damn it!*" Leo pounded his fists on the office table. Anh and Mom both asked what was up.

"Your Samantha is a hunter and has been using you all for information, and she's here now," Isa explained.

"What?" Anh said, shocked.

"Come on." Isa took off her jacket and exposed two scabbards across her back. "Arm yourselves; they'll kill you, too, if I can't stop them."

Pop told Mom and Anh to stay inside as he unlocked a panel in the office wall that had a few ARs mounted with a double-drum magazine. He took one, loaded it, and handed it to Leo.

"That's my baby," he said in the voice of a man who had been broken. Pop said nothing and handed the AR to me instead. I hesitated, then took it.

My mother stood up. "No" was my father's only word, and my mother's response was "Oh, shut up!" as she loaded her own AR. Anh got up and took a pistol that was about as big as she was and sat with her husband. We didn't know what was waiting for us outside until we got close to the door and saw the two drones hovering over the yard with guns pointed at the door.

I-god called Pop. "I just want Isabel, not you; she and Samantha are mine."

Pop hung up. He reached into the back of a cabinet full of glasses. I thought it an odd time for a glass of water. He flipped a switch with a safety cover over it. The next thing we heard was Sam yelling as she dodged a couple of smaller drones that were out of sight as they crashed into the back fence.

"That should really piss I-god off."

"Now, Samantha, your mom and dad are over here. You don't want to risk their getting hurt, do you?"

A burst of gunfire tore through the back door, ripping it mostly off the hinges and sending us to the floor for cover. Glass, bits of wood, smoke, and debris filled the air around us.

When the short burst of fire was done, Sam yelled, "Send her out or I will come get her."

I looked up and saw bits of fluff hovering in the area, and Isa hadn't moved at all. We were covered in debris and she was clean.

"These are stand-alone drones, EMP-hardened. We'll need the big boy I sent you. Where is it?"

"In the car stall in the backyard," Pop said, looking up.

"I'll distract them," Isa said. "Byron, you go get it. Ike and Mrs. Callaway . . . Mrs. Callaway?"

"Call me Helen, dear," she said as she fell back and Pop caught her.

A long thin piece of glass was sticking out just above her belly button, blood flowing from the back; then she went limp in my father's arms.

He laid her down softly.

"Samantha, what have you done?" Pop was out the door!

I turned and opened fire on the armored drone, watching my bullets bounce off as Isa leaped into the air, sending one of her swords into the large drone's front left motor. She retrieved her blade and sent it into the motor behind. This drone had eight rotors and was the size of a car. It could handle losing one motor but not two next to each other. Sam was in the yard and grabbed the piece of pipe she had kicked into the fence wall the night before and threw it. She hit my father in the back, and over the wall she went before I could get a bullet in her direction. Leo was standing over my mother as Anh sat and held her. We watched as my father stumbled to the EMP to arm and charge the weapon with a piece of pipe sticking out of his back. Leo had his own weapon now, and, as Sam reappeared, jumping over the back fence wall and heading toward Pop, we opened fire, sending her back over the fence.

Isa had sent one of the crippled drones crashing into the street and was now trying to avoid tranquilizer fire from the second. It wouldn't be long before more drones were on the way for sure. Isa and I met where my father was with Leo not far behind.

"I'm sorry, brother," Leo said. "I'm here now."

"You're the one that's late this time," Pop said, gasping for air.

We heard a slight scream from inside, and Leo ran back to the house. He quickly emerged, covered in blood. "She was still holding Helen when Sam cut her throat."

Leo took Pop's hand and held it tight. I knelt beside him, and Sam appeared at the other end of the yard with the drone behind her. Isa slid down the roof of the house and landed next to us like a superhero just as the large EMP went off! I could feel the electricity flow across my skin and saw little colorful spots dancing in front of my eyes. The large drone banked slightly, then quickly tried to recover. Sam fell flat to the ground, and Isa dropped to a knee. "Oh my God, that hurts!" Isabel said. The drone started to fire on us, but its aim was off; it was still recovering from the EMP blast.

It launched a net that captured Sam and flew off a bit wobbly, heading east quickly. I looked at Pop and he tried to speak, but there was too much blood. He rolled on his side as he vomited blood and gasped for air. "Tough old dude. I love you, Pop!"

He smiled and was no more.

I was a father; then I wasn't. I was getting married; then I wasn't . . . again! My mother was . . . Isa and Leo helped me up, and I hugged them both. I picked up my and my father's rifles, then led Leo and Isa into the house. The neighbors were at the door and were asking if we needed help.

Mr. Marx and his partner, Jerry, said, "We heard the alarm, Leo. Byron's arc generator began firing, so we turned ours on and made sure the rest of the neighborhood did too."

"Thanks, fellas. You guys, everybody did well, just like we discussed," Leo said. "Hell, you probably saved our lives. We didn't have to deal with a swarm of small drones. Thank you! Samantha is under I-god's control, and she . . ."

Mr. Marx and Jerry hugged Leo tightly.

"I'm okay for now, fellas, thank you. She killed Anh, Helen, and Byron. She . . . we stopped her temporarily, but she will be back. I-god is after something, and I think it doesn't have it yet."

A broken Leo said, "Those small drones needed communication links, and the neighbors, you all were actually able to shut that down. I supplied most of the electrical parts, but I've never seen the arc generator in action. I'm sorry, but we need to go."

Leo said that he would stay and take care of things here and that we should take Pop's Subaru and go to the land he and Pop had been planning to give Sam and me. Isa said that Sam would know where it was, but Leo reassured her that no one but he knew where it was now. It had never changed owners officially, so it couldn't be traced back to them. They'd only seen old pictures of it in a photo album, so there was no digital signature at all. "You'll be traveling north, and the weather is going to be terrible the next couple of days—perfect time to travel unseen. Head south just as the weather hits, then turn north. I-god and Sam will waste a lot of time looking in the wrong direction."

"Leo, what about you? You can't stay here either. She'll kill you too! I-god has control of her now; your Samantha is gone," Isa said.

Leo sighed. "No, my little girl is still in there, but I saw what she did, and I'm no fool. I'll be all right. Now, get cleaned up and packed, and don't be shy. No time for that now. Get moving!"

We went to my parents' room. The back of my shoulder was itching like crazy. I took off my shirt and saw the tear and the blood.

"Hey, Isa."

"I'm on it, Ike. It's not bad, but I'll have to clean and patch it up a bit."

She poured some peroxide on the wound, and I could hear the bubbling and then the sting and burning hit. "Where do they keep the rest of the first aid stuff?"

"Third drawer down."

"Okay, perfect. Come here and let's see what we have. Oh yuck, damn; that's going to be an ugly scar. I'm really sorry about all this, Ike. I should never have come."

"Thanks, Isa, but it's not your fault. You probably saved my life and Leo's too. None of us saw this coming until it was too late. This war is fake, and I-god is building an army of humans so it can move from one or more humans at a time. How did you become a mod?"

"It must have been when I had my appendix surgery."

"Isa, we were in the navy then. I picked you up from the hospital."

"Yes, remember we got there in the morning, and you waited for me that whole time till late that night? Remember, we joked about how long it took? I was so impressed with you that day, I called my mother and told her I had met a really nice guy. She told me to keep both eyes on you until she got to meet you; then she'd let me know if you were really a nice guy."

"I'm sorry. *Ouch!*"

"Sorry, Ike; I have to stitch it. Don't be a baby now! What were you saying?"

"I was saying sorry. I never got to tell you what happened afterward." So I told her the whole story, ending with today.

"Oh my God, what an evil bruja! Well, Ike, good thing I don't like to be second place, just to let you know."

"Ouuuch. Damn, Isa, I'm sorry. So, what are your abilities?"

"I'm not really sure. I just discovered a new one today. I stayed clean; nothing really touched me." *Another lie, Isabel. Why am I lying to him? Why should I trust him?*

"I think that may be a form of push. If it is, then you're a mod and a god! No wonder I-god wants you so bad."

"Oh, so it's not because I'm cute? Oh, and don't say anything funny; I want to stay mad at you still."

My wound was stitched, and I let her shower first.

"Stop being shy like Leo said, and keep your eyes and hands to yourself." She told me to turn around so she could scrub the bits of wood and glass out of my back. She told me to check her back just in case, and wow, not a scratch, just a small scar at the curve of her lower back.

"What's this scar from back here?"

"What scar, where?" She took my hand. "Show me." She put my hand on the top of her butt on that lovely curve. Samantha was a beautiful woman, but Isabel was beautiful and had a gorgeous curvy body.

I rubbed my finger on her scar and then put her fingers on it.

"Hurry up in there!" we heard from outside. There was a lot of activity inside and outside the house.

Isa quickly turned and faced me, her breasts against my chest; she took a step back, looked down, and smiled. "Very nice, Isaac. Now let's go; we're losing time."

We dressed and came out of the room, her shoulder-length hair still wet. Leo had our bags packed and the car loaded. We went dark, and he gave each of us a map. He said that if either one of us ever got tortured, we couldn't tell what we didn't know; the two halves made a whole.

We hugged Leo and thanked the neighbors. They told us how much they loved my parents and that they would see that everything was taken care of.

"I'll drive the first part of the trip heading south; you need to get some rest," Isa said. "You're not okay right now, but you have to be. I need you to drive through the storm that's coming, Isaac."

"I'll be all right, Isabel; I'll be just fine."

I was drained yet determined to get revenge. We got into Pop's Subaru, and off we went. We didn't talk as Isabel drove (and ate like she was starving). I sank into the passenger seat and was asleep in no time.

ACKNOWLEDGMENTS

Music was—and remains—a great inspiration and creative force in my life; without it my life would not be possible.

DAY TWO—THE HUNTER

The woman's been found; she is the Hunter.

Was I too mentally exhausted to cry or still in shock? Was it that my heart had been ripped out and stomped on, again, or was it how it got shoved back into my chest and I just had to deal with my new reality? I wouldn't ever see my parents again, and it was the woman I loved who had betrayed me again and flaunted in my face a child who was supposed to be mine. I was so angry! I was so heartbroken and felt so lost at this moment, lost and alone, staring at the woman I denied and had been in love with just to honor a commitment. Why! Damn it, why! I saw the life leave both of my parents today, watched things that should not be possible happen, and I didn't have my father's wisdom to help me. I never had many friends—just Sam, Isabel, and Chris.

I watched the tears fall from Isabel's eyes, and she said, "Sorry." That was it! I'm glad the car was stopped, because the tears that I couldn't find had found me. She held me as I sobbed, snot bubbles and all; it was everything coming out all at once. I tried to stop, and I think that just made things worse. I stepped out of the car into the cold rain and thought of my father's body lying outside and my mother in a mangled house that she kept so meticulously clean for as long as I can remember. I fell to the ground and cried in the rain for what seemed an eternity. Then something my grandmother said to me when I was little popped into my head.

"Crying don't fix nothing, son. The more you cry, the less you pee is all, so stop crying and get to gettin'."

I remember her hugging me, kissing me on both cheeks, and smiling that grandmother smile that just makes everything better. I stood up, holding on to that memory as Isabel got out of the car and switched positions with me. There was a piece of paper in the door pocket. It was a note from Leo.

I'm so sorry, Isaac. No one should have to endure what you must be going through now.

Now get your ass over to your father's favorite car shop. You know who to see.

Tell him what happened, and he'll know what to do from there.

You don't have much time to get where you're going, and I-god will be looking for you.

Don't let I-god get Isabel, and don't you get caught yet.

I'll see you in a couple of weeks. The trails need to get really cold.

Stay out of sight. I'll have some answers when I get there.

Isabel is probably not going to tell you everything. Get over it now.

Love you, son, and don't do anything stupid!

I read the note out loud, and Isabel said, "I'll tell you what I know, Ike."

We got to the car audio shop in La Jolla just as the storm was really picking up. We ran in, and Mac, Pop's old army and car buddy, was there. We started telling him what happened, and Mac stopped us. He said to pull the car in right away first. We continued telling the story as he gathered some tools.

"Your father and I think that I-god tracks our vehicles electronically, by sight and sound. Drive the car onto that lift."

Mac unbolted the loudish aftermarket catback exhaust and replaced it with a stock WRX exhaust system he had leaning in a corner of the shop.

"Your father's idea, Isaac—we're going to plasti-dip your car, too, add a black accent on your hood, and also hit that roof. Get your stuff out of the car, all of it."

"Why?" Isabel asked.

"Young lady, I'm not one to explain what I do, but I-god is looking for you two, right? How long do you think a little paint and new exhaust system will fool it? Now, move your shit!"

Isabel was hot. I looked at her, shook my head. She rolled her eyes so hard, Mac couldn't help but notice. He ignored her anyway.

"Mac, what car will we be taking?"

"You have a choice—the black Accord or the Accord that's black!" This brought a bit of a smile to his gruff face as he wiped a few tears from his eyes. "Go have a look. It's my little project. Keys are on the seat," Mac said, trying to hold his voice steady.

I saw Isabel's eyes begin to fill with tears too.

"All you men crying is just too much," she said.

I popped the hood, and there was a small frunk!

Mac was walking toward us and smiling. "I was planning on whooping your father's ass again at the racetrack now I have a freaking Subaru and you have an AWD Tesla-powered 2008 Accord coupe. I bet he planned this somehow, damn it! You can't be on the run and stopping for gas now, can you? It's a fully dark vehicle, no GPS, Wi-Fi, etcetera. It does have an encrypted two-way radio, but don't use it for more than thirty seconds—the content is secure, but the signal can be tracked. We have a few dummy transmitters scattered about, but we figure they'll buy only thirty seconds of talk time, max. Young lady, I'm sorry about snapping at you earlier. Byron was my friend." Mac's voice broke a bit, and a few tears fell from his eyes.

Isabel hugged Mac. "I'm sorry for not trusting you, Mr. Mac."

"It's just Mac, and who are you, young lady? I'm not sure where Isaac's manners are right now."

I was not expecting that from Mac, nor was I expecting this old Accord to be so damn cool!

"I'm sorry, Mac. This is Isabel, Isabel, Mac. He is the master builder my father always goes . . . went to."

Mac smiled and replied, "Very nice to meet you, Isabel. I wish you had time to tell me how such a beautiful young lady got wrapped up and stuck with this kid. Oh well, let me show you everything she can do and get you all out the door."

Mac loaded Isabel's bag onto the back seat and showed us the solar generator in the trunk and the rolls of panels. Of course, there was also a massive JL w7 lurking on a baffle board running free air!

"She's got a Model S P85D dual motor setup, and those panels can give you about three, maybe three point five kilowatts of charging, so it will take two to three days of full sun to recharge a depleted battery. Where you'll be going, there will be plenty of solar and batteries to quick charge and probably a few backups as well. I helped your father design the system, but I don't know where this place is. He and I imagined that would be best. All these streetlights and telephone poles have gunshot-detection systems. They are just directional microphones used to triangulate the position of a gunshot. Your pop and I figured that I-god may be using what it knows about us to track us in detail. Oh, and don't play your weird music either; there are microphones, and I-god knows what you like to listen to. You two are stuck talking to each other until you get out of town. Oh, here's a map of the cameras and microphones. Most have been sabotaged, but I-god works fast repairing them."

"Thank you, Mac, but what the hell is going on? My fiancée killed my mom and her own, tried to kill me, and is knocked up by I-god. *What the hell is going on?* Please!"

"In a war, there are refugees even if there is genocide. There have been no refugees, Isaac. Your pop and I thought that this war was made up, not real at all. A few explosions here and there, some destroyed drones, and a few tales of won and lost battles given by who exactly? That's bullshit, man! Look, we didn't quite figure out exactly what I-god is up to or why it would fake a war and create a fake villain. We figured it was hiding a real genocide; the extinction of humanity, or trying to get itself into human form. Our team debated which one made the most sense; your father and I thought, *Why not both things.*"

"We think I-god has gotten into a human and is trying to transfer itself from a digital life-form to another form, a biological one," Isabel added. "We think it wants to live forever, and life-forms on Earth have a pretty good record of sticking around in one form or another. We also think that it wants to go off-world to improve its chances of immortality."

"Wait, wait, wait. You mean to tell me this stuff is really possible and not just sci-fi bull?"

"Look at me, Isaac; look at me! Do I exist? Does Sam exist? You saw and heard her change, and she's not the first or only one."

"You're a mod?" Mac said. "What can you do?"

"I can kick your ass," she said with a smirk. "I'm still learning; I'm fast, strong, and nothing seems to touch my skin."

Mac smacked her hand and said, "Well, that power sucks!"

"*Ouch, Abuelo, tus viejas y sucias manos lastiman.*"

"My hands are clean."

Isabel replied, "It doesn't work that way; something has to be moving fast and be dangerous and stuff, not just nasty."

Mac got a good laugh out of that. "Your powers still suck!"

ABOUT THE AUTHOR

Chancellor Brown is a US Navy veteran who served for eight and a half years and in two wars. He has worked in high technology for over three decades. Brown grew up just outside of Washington, DC, in Fort Washington, Maryland, and he currently lives in Escondido, California, with his wife and two sons. *The Singularity* is his debut novel.